THE DEADLY ADMIRER

MARTIN VAN HELDEN

ISBN: 978-1-923512-65-8 (Paperback)

 A catalogue record for this book is available from the National Library of Australia

Cover Design: Author name and Clark & Mackay
Format and Typeset: Author name and Clark & Mackay
Published by Author name and Clark & Mackay

Proudly printed in Australia by Clark & Mackay

DEAR READER.

Congratulations on your purchase and many thanks from me Author Martin van Helden and my team.

Reading can be very relaxing and can help you find new ideas and you can take your book wherever you go at any time of the day.

I hope you will enjoy this book and be inspired to read my other books too.

With the highest respect,

Martin van Helden.
Author

CHAPTER 1

CATHERINE'S BLUE EYES slowly opened. It was calm. Beautifully calm, she thought with a soft smile, just before her alarm went off. The beeping sound was quite annoying, but it did the job of telling her it was time to get her butt up.

Devi whimpered next to her, as she rolled over her king-sized bed to reach for the clock. Her little puppy hated the sound of the alarm, way more than she did. She barked angrily at the clock, making Catherine giggle.

"Happy now?" Catherine asked, as the silence was restored.

With another bark, Devi laid back, and closed her eyes. Sure enough, as Catherine got out of bed, slipping her feet into warm fluffy slippers, Devi was next to her. Her dog loved to go through with her on her morning routine.

Covering a yawn, Catherine pulled the curtains open, ushering in the bright rays of light of the Florida morning. She sighed in contentment, taking in a long drawl of the warm air as she stepped out into her wide balcony that overlooked the pool below.

Despite being her view for over three years, she could not help but marvel at how beautiful it was from up here every morning. It was her ritual daily, to stand right here and take all of it in, the beauty of nature she called her home. She had bought this house for that very reason, the tree lines that not only gave her privacy from her other wealthy neighbors, but the nature that reminded her of the ranch she had spent most of her childhood.

She giggled as Devi yapped excitedly. Her dog like her loved the nature. She could sense her excitement whenever they headed outside, as she waited for the go ahead to race off on an adventure.

A blast of chill hit her, and she pulled at the lapels of her silky coat, leaving the doors open as she returned to her room to get started for the day.

The huge bathroom had been a delight working the design with the interior designer. A huge bathtub, which was one of her favorite places to spend the evenings. Bottles of soaps and creams lined the table, and she reached for her favorite scent, strawberry, sighing as the aroma soon overwhelmed the room.

In a blue towel, she strutted into her walk in-closet. It had been another selling point for the house, with a much larger space than most of the offers on the market. "It is going to be more than enough," the agent had said with conviction.

Catherine giggled. Every shelf and row were occupied by a dress, shoe, bag, makeup or just something else. She had decluttered just three months ago, clearing out bags of designers, and yet it was back to being filled up. She consciously jotted it on her to-do-list to call Abby, her personal shopper to come around for a more intense round of decluttering.

She stood in front of her underwear closet. It was filled with her babies as she liked to call them. For the past five years, she mostly wore Caths, her lingerie brand. Who better than herself to promote her business? Caths was a simple idea – make women comfortable in their underwear and it was over almost a million-dollar worth as at today. Incredible! It was the start of a new week, and what better way than to be clothed in black lacey underwear?

She smiled as the lace of the fabric caressed her body. She caught her reflection in the mirror. Her tall, or as many in the fashion industry said, her long body was perfection, her pale completion a beautiful contrast to the black lingerie. She giggled as she did a twirl, Devi yapping in approval. She did a little strut, laughing at how silly she was as she waved at the imaginary audience.

Her outfit of the day had been picked out last night after a look at her calendar. Lots of meetings to attend today so she was going with a brown power suit, designed by Dolce. It was a definite choice as she admired her look in front of the floor length mirror.

Catherine Miles was a magazine front page delight. At 6'2, her long legs drifted up in well-tailored trousers, her feet encased in red Louboutin. Her body had come with a beautiful face, long and symmetrical with gorgeous eyes and flawless skin. Many said she was blessed with a pretty face and body. And those plump lips? They were a delight on the cover of magazines. She flashed a smile at herself in the mirror. She was good to go… well, not yet.

She took a few steps towards a shelf, pulling at the door which exposed an array of bottles from top to bottom. These were her scents, from different cultures around the world. The top row, however, was covered with her own personal scents, from her brand, Cat Scents. She had always been attracted to smells, owning a perfume line was something she had always known she would do. But it was not until last year it had come into fruition after years of research and working with the lab. She loved and owned every single scent in her brand. Every single one, proudly basking herself in them.

The cold liquid melted against her wrist as she pressed the button. Chocolate. The aroma drifted to her, and she moaned in contentment. Then she reached for another bottle. This was of Oud fragrance, and she pumped it on her neck.

As she stepped back in front of the mirror, she smiled with the realization that she was ready for the day. Well, that was after breakfast.

Devi circled around her excitedly as they headed downstairs. The aroma of freshly brewed coffee drifted to her as she walked into the kitchen. Making scrambled eggs was Tehila, her chef and housekeeper. She was an older woman, in her fifties, and dotted on Catherine.

"Good morning, Catherine. Hope you rested well," Tehila smiled as she poured coffee into a teacup for her.

"Yes, I did," Catherine said. The weekend had been busy, but she had gotten her beauty rest, and was ready to get started with the week. "Thanks," she said, as Tehila placed a cup of coffee and plate of scrambled egg and toast in front of her. "Sorry Tehila, but I have to get going," she said.

"Busy day today?"

Catherine shook her head. Once upon a time, she had struggled with having a work-life balance, but now, she had free time. Too much free time, she must admit. And that was something that needed to be dealt with.

"I should be home by noon," Catherine said. "If something doesn't come up," she added quickly as Tehila flashed her a sad smile.

"I will be here waiting. With Devi," Tehila said. Hearing her name, Devi jumped excitedly, wagging her tail.

Kissing goodbye to Devi, Catherine headed towards the garage. In there were parked her two cars, a white Porsche, and white Range Rover. Yes, white was her favorite color. There was just something so warm and peaceful about it, that she let herself be surrounded by the hue most of the time.

Devi barked excitedly as she got into the car. "See you later!" she waved as the engine of the Range Rover came alive. The doors of the garage opened, and she sped off, headed for the city.

CHAPTER 2

A TAYLOR SWIFT song played as Catherine headed into town. Usually, she would sing out her heart to the lyrics, but her mind was occupied. At thirty-eight, Catherine had a lot going on. The decline had begun about twelve years ago, then work began to slow down. The companies had wanted younger models, who were more in tune with the fashion industry. At that time, she had delved into her lingerie business, and two years later, her perfume business. It hadn't been much of a sting, but the past five years had her witness the least calls. The truth was, her career as a model was drying up, and she refused to accept it. She was just thirty-eight, and there were models twenty years older than her who had more limelight.

It wasn't as if she didn't put herself out there. She did! She socialized and made friends with the right people. She was still gorgeous, and her body rivalled some of those younger girls. It hurt more than she wanted to admit. Modelling was a lifelong career to her, well until she was old and grey. But she was still in her prime and refused to be discarded. When she did leave the modelling industry, it was going to be on her own terms, with her not being forced out.

She sighed. She was not going to give up. Not now. Not ever. She had worked too hard to get to where she was.

She pulled up in front of Eclipse, an intimate restaurant. It was her usual hang out spot, and the staff always welcomed her. Even if there was a crowd, they created a space for her. It was almost empty at the time of the day, on a Monday. She waved at the hostess, and headed to the patio table which was her favorite.

She opened the menu and flipped it open. She had just had a cup of coffee and needed to have breakfast. As she pondered over the menu, she felt a shadow overhead. A smile appeared on her face as she looked up to see Max Overland, her manager and friend.

Max was a good-looking man. In his forties, he was tall, with a lean and broad built, gotten from working out intensely at the gym. His dark long hair had a scattering of grey, and his face was gorgeous, with dark eyes which could hold someone in a trance. It was a wonder he had never delved into modeling in his youth; he would have been a favorite. He was a charming man, and had charmed his way into being Catherine's manager for the past five years. They had met at a charity event. At that point, her former manager, Riley had quit to relocate with his wife who had cancer to Europe. She had been lost, wondering what to do. And the gentleman had slid next to her, and introduced himself formally to her, offering his services as her manager.

Max was not just a charming gentleman. He delivered with his work, and had landed her contracts after tough negotiations with big brands like Omega and Nike. When it had seemed she had hit rock bottom, he had pulled her out, landing her massive sponsorship that stirred her career towards a solid path.

"Max," she smiled as she kissed him on the cheek.

"Catherine. You look lovely as ever," Max said in a deep voice, returning her smile.

"I ordered the omelet for you," she said. It was his usual breakfast here.

He nodded absently, and she frowned. There was something off about him. Usually, he would rave on about how amazing the egg was. "Is everything okay?" Catherine swallowed, as her heart began to race fast in fear. Ten years ago, she had had a similar moment with Riley, as he sat her down and told her he couldn't be her manager anymore.

"Of course. How are you doing?"

"Okay, I guess," Catherine shrugged.

"And business?"

Catherine sighed. Owning two businesses was a huge responsibility financially. As much as she loved being a businesswoman, she had put in a lot of her savings, and it was still taking a while to get her returns. She was proud of what she had accomplished with her business, bringing her dreams alive, but it wasn't all that glittery. Pre COVID, and her businesses had been doing well, with enough profit. But after the pandemic, they were struggling just enough to meet with expenses, with a little to take home. The cost of raw materials had gone up, and competition in the market had increased. She was working hard to stay afloat.

"Hiring a consultant to come in," Catherine said. This was going to set her back thousands of dollars, but a consultant was highly needed to look at her business through the eyes of a third party, and provide her with the necessary changes she needed to implement to succeed. "Max, I am worried. I can't recall the last time I got a huge gig. I mean the last one was the one with Nike for the clothing brand, and they didn't renew the contract. And that was like almost a year ago. I need something big. Not just one, or two, but a whole lot," Catherine confessed.

Max nodded in agreement, casting a look over his shoulder. She followed his gaze, resting on a waiter who walked past. "I know Catherine, and I am working on it," Max said.

There he went again. He had never been one for a few words. Something was wrong. "What's going on?"

"Instagram models, market is oversaturated. Every tall skinny girl thinks she's a model, and is willing to take a dollar and a pair of shoes to strut the runway or pose in front of a camera. And then the bloody influencers," Max sighed. "They are everywhere on social media."

"I am an influencer," Catherine pointed out.

Max chuckled. "You know what I mean. These kids are all over social media, getting gifts, and creating a large followership which they can influence to buy whatever they promote. We need to explore that route, Catherine."

Catherine sighed. She wasn't much of a social media user. Max had been the one to open an Instagram account for her years ago, and she had to admit it did boost her business sales. For her, she wasn't one to put her life out there for all to see. It was why she had turned down offers to be on reality shows. But she did see people doing so well on social media. Literally anything could be sold on there. It was cult-like, with fans, buying whatever celebrities pushed at them. A couple of brands had approached her in the past to influence for them, but she was wary of doing so, and only went with very few brands. She didn't want to influence people wrongly.

"It has to happen Catherine. Keys wants you to be their global ambassador, but they need you to advertise for them on social media," Max said.

Keys was a luxury jewelry brand that Catherine had worked with in the past. They had rebranded and were taking the market by storm, with an appeal to the younger generation.

"Fine. Let's do this," Catherine said. If putting herself out there would steer her career on the right path, so be it.

"Great. I will reach out to them. I also have a couple of other offers lined up. You know I am only aiming for the best for you Catherine," Max said.

Catherine smiled. Max had shown all through the years that he had her best interests at heart. She trusted him to ensure that her rights were protected. He would not put her in a situation that would get her in trouble. He understood her principles, and only got her projects that aligned with them.

"Thank you, Max," Catherine smiled.

Max glanced at his watch. "I have to get going now," he said as he stood up.

"But you haven't even touched your breakfast," Catherine nodded at his untouched meal. He had only taken a few sips of his coffee.

"Had an early breakfast," he said, flashing a quick smile at her. "I have a couple of errands to run. I will send the details of Keys to you once I formalize with them. I will see you Cath." He leaned over and quickly kissed her, before dashing off as if he couldn't wait to be away from her.

Her eyes followed him with a frown until he was out of view. What was up with him? He had other clients, but he always dedicated time to her. They had more than a manager and client relationship. They had become friends. Perhaps, it was just a busy day, but even then, he had seemed out of it, flustered, his mind far away. She would call him later in the week to find out what was wrong with him, she decided.

After breakfast, Catherine headed to her office which was a couple of minutes away. As she pulled into the driveway of the building, a smile crept on her face as she read the sign up on the building Cathy Place.

She grabbed her bag and headed in. Inside was a small boutique of lingerie. There was another room to the side where the bottles of perfume were showcased. There was also a dressing room where shoppers could try on their lingerie.

Her perfumes were made in a lab in Venice and shipped down for sales here in Florida, and also distributed to other stores. Her lingerie was made in Italy and shipped down as well. The shop had few stocks as shipments were sent out to retail stores around the country where most of the revenue came from.

"Good morning, Catherine," Natalie said. She was the front desk receptionist and was quite a free bird. She always wore a burst of colors, and was a bright addition.

"Hi Nat. How was your date?" Catherine asked.

"It was dreadful," Natalie groaned. In her late twenties, Natalie had just left a five-year relationship, and had launched herself into the dating pool, which was certainly filled with sharks. "He had his hands all over me, all through the date. I almost stabbed him with a fork," Natalie said with a shudder.

Catherine chuckled at Natalie's disgust. "I am sorry you had to go through that," she sympathized.

"You have no idea how lucky you are not to be bothered with all of this," Natalie said.

Well, she was wrong. Catherine was heading into her forties, and she was single. Never been married either, and she didn't have a kid. It wasn't for lack of trying though. She had been in relationships in the past, but it had never been enough for her to head to the aisle. And she could not help but wonder at times if she shouldn't have settled when she was younger. As much as she had a lot going for her, she felt lonely most of the time. It would be great to have a partner to keep her warm in the night, and to have kids running around.

"Henry is at the back," Natalie rolled her eyes.

Henry was a wannabe actor. He was in his early twenties and was the customer service and social media handler for the business. He was a jovial kid, who wanted to be an actor and Catherine was pretty sure that one day he was going to catch his break.

"Well, I will be in my office if you or anyone needs me," Catherine said, as she headed down the hall.

She had a small office, which she totally loved, with a not so amazing view of the parking lot of the next building. She went through the mail, mostly made up of bills, which she would have to pay. She made a point to attend to them before the end of the week. She went through her calendar, taking note of the shoots and meetings she had during the week. Barely any, but at least it was something. She trusted Max to come up with more jobs before the end of the month, so she would have her calendar booked. She smiled sadly as she recalled those days when she was fully booked, with barely any free time. From one shoot, she was onto the next. There were nights she was kept awake with energy drinks filled with caffeine. Days she had cameras flashing in her face, in what seemed to be like no end. Whewh! At that point, she had wanted a break from all the chaos, but right now she would trade her long and empty days for those days.

"YOU ARE LATE." Catherine frowned as she opened the front door. Her best friend, Megan smiled broadly, as if that would take away the fact that she was over thirty minutes late.

"I am so sorry Cathie, a last-minute work meeting came up," Megan said as she strolled into the house.

Megan Holmes was Catherine's best friend, one of the few people Catherine had let into her private circle. She was the girl next door, as Catherine was fond of saying, but Megan considered herself forgettable with her simple black hair which was now in a bob, and dark eyes. She had a gorgeous body, curvy in all the right places that turned eyes when Megan wore a tight-dress, which she never wore, since she was always in those ugly office suits.

Of all the relationships in the world, Catherine held hers and Megan in high esteem. She had gone through ups and downs with her, and could not even imagine not having her as a friend.

"You should quit you know," Catherine said as she handed her a glass of wine.

They were having lunch out by the pool, which was prepared by Tehila. It was their weekly routine whenever Megan was in town; to have lunch and catch up.

Megan chuckled as she shrugged out of her jacket, tossing it on a chair which made Catherine grimace. That was a designer which she had picked out for Megan, but trust her friend not to have an iota of what luxury meant. But then, Megan was a former tomboy, and still one at heart.

Megan worked in corporate. It was a tough job that required her presence and attention most of the time. She was always so damn busy, and overworked, that Catherine could not help but be pissed. When last had her friend gone on a holiday huh?

"You need a break," Catherine said, staring at Megan. There were bags underneath her eyes.

"I know," Megan covered a yawn. "But work is so crazy right now. We are short-staffed you know."

Catherine rolled her eyes. Megan had been giving her this same excuse for the past two years. They were short-staffed? Then hire more!

"We should go on a vacation. Even if it is just for the weekend, you need some time to rest Megan," Catherine said.

"How's work going?" Megan said. As expected, she had diverted the attention from herself to Catherine. It was a technique Catherine was used to, and overtime, Megan didn't even bother hiding her attempts. Megan was much of a private person, and steered attention from herself, letting Catherine take the limelight.

Catherine sighed. "If I don't get something substantial, I might be broke by the end of the year."

Megan patted her leg. "It's not going to get that bad Cathie," she consoled.

Catherine hoped so. She had seen the last invoice of production and had almost fainted. The inflation rate was driving the cost of materials high, giving the consumer less purchasing power.

"If you need a loan, let me know huh?" Megan flashed a smile.

"Got a million you could give to me?" Catherine teased with a chuckle.

Megan's phone rang and she frowned as she stared at it. Catherine lifted a brow as she turned off her phone.

"A suitor?" she teased.

Megan rolled her eyes. "What are we? In the thirteenth century?"

"You still haven't answered the question," Catherine pointed out. To the best of her knowledge, Megan wasn't seeing someone, but then they hadn't seen each other in person in about two weeks, and that was a lot of time to meet someone.

"No. Just someone I am not interested in talking to. At least right now," Megan said with a faraway look in her eyes.

Catherine really wished Megan would open up more to her. As much as her friend was outgoing and confident, lately, she felt that she was keeping a lot from her. Yes, she knew a lot of her secrets, but she felt Megan held back, even though she denied it. Lately, it felt like there was something going on with Megan, and she wasn't sharing.

"How's Dave doing? It's been a while," Catherine asked, referring to Megan's foster brother. Megan had grown up in foster care after being abandoned by her mother. Those years had been tough for her, as the foster family she had grown up with had been cutthroats who hadn't given a damn about the kids under their care. This had motivated Megan to get out of the gutter, or shithole as she often said. She had done well in her high school, despite the limited resources and had gotten a scholarship to an Ivy League. She and Dave had been the closest at the foster home they had grown up in; their relationship continuing to bloom even after Megan had left for college.

"I guess he's doing great. Haven't spoken to him in a while," Megan said.

Over the years, the siblings had drifted apart, with Catherine taking center place in Megan's life. This Christmas, Catherine planned to throw a party, and invite Dave over, so the siblings could catch up on the old times.

"Are you sure you are okay? You have me worried," Catherine said concerned.

Megan flashed her a smile, but she could tell it wasn't genuine. "Yes, I am fine," Megan reassured her.

They definitely needed that vacation, Catherine decided right there. Somehow, she was going to make arrangements for her and Megan to have some quiet and girl time. She was not going to take no for an answer. If it was going to take her marching to Megan's office to get her some time off, she would do so, but her friend needed some time away from her chaotic work and the crazy life of Florida.

She smiled broadly. Yes, she didn't know where, or when although it had to be some time soon, but they were going on a girl's trip.

"Why do you have that mischievous look on your face?" Megan asked suspiciously.

Catherine responded by smiling even wider, as she began to deliberate over their vacation plans.

"Move to the side," Larry's sharp voice pulled Catherine out of her thoughts. She threw him a look, why was he shouting and glaring at her? However, she did as instructed, taking a few steps to the left, while still maintaining her position with her hand on her waist. The camera lights went off as she stared into the distance.

How much longer was this going to take because she needed to call Max. She had no idea why but all through yesterday he had been on her mind. She had tried calling him last night, but his number had been unavailable. She had done the same this morning, and it was still unavailable. This was odd. Max always had his phone line open.

"Catherine, can you focus?" Larry snapped.

She flashed an apologetic smile to him as she retained her position. How many more pictures did he need to take again? Because she wanted to give Max another call.

"That's a wrap," Larry said.

"Whewh!" She got down from the raised platform of the studio. She loved being in front of the camera, but today she was just not in the mood.

"Catherine, we need to talk," Larry frowned.

"Okay," she smiled.

He looked around the studio. They were not alone. The make-up artist was present, as well as the assistant photographer and the creative director for Elim, the brand she was doing the shoot for.

"I haven't given the pictures a thorough look, but I may have to do a reshoot," Larry said.

"What? Why!" she cried out. She hated reshoots. Standing in the same position? Doing probably the same makeup, and the same props? They were dreadful. "Let me see the pictures," she said as he handed over the camera to her. Not a stranger to one, she scrolled through the pictures he had taken and grimaced.

"You were distracted," Larry pointed out.

Yeah, that was clear to her in the couple of pictures she saw. She had that faraway look in her eyes, with no focus in view.

"Is everything okay?" Larry asked.

She nodded. "Sorry about that, had a long day yesterday. Let me know if we are going to have a reshoot," Catherine sighed. Now she was in a bad mood. Time and effort seemed to have been wasted, and it was her fault. As well as Max. If only his number was available, she wouldn't have to worry so much, right?

She headed to the restroom and shrugged out of her shoot outfit. In front of the mirror, she grabbed a wipe from a basket and removed the makeup from her face. She wasn't one for makeup, getting rid of it immediately the purpose was done. Her skin underneath was soft, translucent and spotless, a result of her investing in skincare in her younger years.

Her phone buzzed in her purse and she quickly reached for it. Max had finally called back, right? Without looking at the screen, she answered the call.

"Hi Max, I have been so worried about you. What's going on?" she blurted out.

There was no response. It was then she pulled away from the phone, and realized it wasn't Max who had called. It was an unknown number which was not saved as a contact.

"Hello? Who is this?" she asked. Still, there was no response, but she could hear voices in the background. She could barely make out what they were saying. A couple of make voices, none of which belonged to Max, and was that a female's voice?

"Max?" she called out.

Her eyes widened at a scream on the other end. What on earth was that?

"Hello? Is everything okay?" She was greeted with a dial tone. What the fuck! She jumped at the knock on the door, realizing her heart was breaking fast. "Who's there?" she called out.

"Larry," he responded.

"I will be out in a second," she called back. She stared at the mirror. Was it just her imagination or there were bags underneath her eyes? She shuddered at the thought. Hell no! She quickly washed her face and dried it with a towel, then headed out.

Larry was the only one left behind, as he packed up his cameras for the next shoot which was going to be out of the studio.

"Hey," she smiled weakly at him.

"I don't think we will be needing a reshoot. A few shots can be used," he said.

She sighed in relief. "Thanks," she said gratefully.

"Are you okay? Everything good?" Larry asked with concern, staring at her intensely.

"Yeah, yeah, I am," Catherine said.

He didn't look like he believed her. She had had a working relationship with Larry for over twelve years. About two decades ago, he used to be a star in the photography field, taking on models and celebrities. He was really good at his work, but just like her, the younger folks were getting all the attention, but she still worked with him, trusting his expertise. In a way, she considered him a friend.

"You are going home, right?" he asked. Catherine nodded. "Let me drive you home." He extended his hands for her keys.

Catherine chuckled. She wasn't down that bad, come on. "Really, I am fine Larry. I can take care of myself," she said. For most of her life, she took care of herself. Through the thick and thin, she had realized it was up to her to defend and protect her world. She couldn't count on anyone but herself. "I will see you on Friday," Catherine said, referring to another shoot she had with him at the end of the week.

"Come relaxed!" Larry called to her.

She smiled as she waved off at him. As she walked out to the car park, she found herself throwing frantic looks over her shoulders, even though the car park was out in the open, and it was broad daylight.

She sat in the driver's seat of the Porsche for a couple of minutes, taking deep breaths. As she stared down at her hands, she realized she was visibly shaken, and this upset her. She was clearly overreacting right? But that scream, it had been a cry for help. Or had it been a cry of pain? It still sent chills all over her body. It had sounded like someone was being hurt. Tortured!

She stared at her phone screen, and reluctantly dialed the number that had called her earlier. She wasn't surprised when she got the operator's message that it was switched off. A part of her hoped it was switched off, because she was worried about what to expect if her call got answered. But wouldn't she like to know what that scream had been about?

She closed her eyes and took a deep breath. Yeah, she was just overreacting. Stress. Sadness. Mid-life crisis. Perhaps she needed to go on a vacation and clear her head or something. But then, when she returned, the bills would still be piled up, she would still have to return to her slow life. Right now, she needed to work hard to remain on track, otherwise she would fall off. She stared long into the distance. Max was fine. He probably had a lot going on, just like she had with herself. When he felt up to it, he would reach out to her. The call had been from a wrong number certainly. Probably it had been a child who had screamed. Or a woman in labor. Yes, that had to be the explanation. She was not going to worry herself anymore, she decided as she put up a weak smile.

Catherine was in the middle of yoga when Max called. She grabbed her phone immediately when she saw his name on the screen.

"Max! Where the hell have you been?" she cried, earning glares from the other patrons in the yoga studio.

"I have been here?" Max said.

"I have been trying to call you since last week. Your number has been unavailable," she accused.

"Silence and calm are integral," the yogi was saying, sending her a look.

Flashing her an apologetic look, Catherine staggered up and left the room for some privacy, before she got booted out.

"I had a couple of things to do out of town, and the cellular network wasn't stable," Max said. "Anything new happened?"

She was about to tell him about the strange call from an unknown number when she stopped herself. He would tell her she was overreacting. No need to make a mountain hole out of it.

"Just same old," Catherine shrugged.

"We are good to go with Keys. Will be sending over the contract later in the day. Be ready Catherine. You asked and I am about to deliver. The next couple of months are going to be busy. Gotten a couple of events, shows and sponsorships lined up for you," Max said.

A broad smile spread on her lips as she did a fist bump. Yes! Max would always deliver. "Thanks Max," she said excitedly.

"Anything for you," Max said.

She giggled as the call ended. Her little giggles grew into a full-blown laugh. A woman who was changing in the locker room gave her a concerned look. Catherine dabbed the tears that had rolled down her eyes. Whewh! It was clear to her that she had been over-reacting. Max was perfectly fine, and well, so would her career. She did a little excited dance for the busy weeks ahead. She couldn't wait!

They wore ready to leave for a short (work) Holyday to Cannes in the south of France Catherine is excited as her best friend Megan joins her as well as Max, but he will be a few days later.

They take her Car to go to the airport as they arrived the Privat jet is waiting on a packed ramp, The captain greets them and says no problem we have you out here in no time. They board the plane and sit in the nice soft leather seats while having a cocktail in VIP class style.

The ringing in her ears ceased as the plane began to taxi down the runway. Catherine opened her eyes, her heartbeat relaxing. She loved flying, except for one thing, the ringing sensation in her ear at takeoff and descending. It made her heartbeat fast in panic.

CHAPTER

"**WELCOME TO THE** Cannes, we hope you have a lovely time here," the pilot said, welcoming them to the beautiful French city.

Catherine smiled as she took off her eye mask. They had the full VIP class, and her window seat had given her an awesome view of the city she had just arrived in. In a few minutes, they were off the plane, and she held on to her Louise-Vuitton carry-on bag, while her other bags are loaded from the private jet into the luggage van that will follow them to the hotel.

A black limousine-van reserved for VIP class awaited them and she got in, putting a pair of sunglasses over her eyes. She switched on her phone and sent a text to Megan. "Just touched down Cannes. See you in a bit!"

Immigration was an easy breeze, and she even got to sign an autograph of one of the attendants, who was a huge fan.

Her driver was Philip, a tall French man with sunburned skin and a wide smile. "Bonjour! Bonjour! Welcome to Cannes," he said excitedly as he took her small bags. "First time in Cannes?" he asked as the car pulled out of the curb.

"No, been here a couple of times," Catherine said.

"You here for business or pleasure?" he grinned wider.

Catherine chuckled. "Both actually." She was supposed to be here for work, an advertising gig with a winery that would last for two or three days. And well, she had decided to give herself a little holiday after wrapping up the gig. Why not spend the rest of the week vacationing in Cannes? It was a great idea for Megan who also needed a break from her chaotic 9-5. She would be flying in later in the evening to join her.

Max was also coming on the trip, but he was going to be a couple of days late. He was currently in Dubai, negotiating a deal for her with one of the luxurious hotels in Dubai. She really hoped the deal would come through. That would not only mean a new source of income for her, but more exposure. If she could break into the market out there, then she was going to have more endorsements and deals.

"You going to enjoy this trip a lot," the man assured her.

Catherine hoped so. The past month has been really busy for her, but she could not complain. Rather busy, than a dull and free spell. She had had shows, interviews, adverts, and even influencing gigs, which had put her out there, growing her followers on social media to almost half a million. It wasn't that bad, but it was a great deal of work responding to her fans. She had had to hire a social media account just to handle her pages, because she just couldn't deal. Henry had let her know point blank that the last message she wanted to portray was that of a snobbish model.

"You need to interact with them. Let them know that you care and that they matter to you, even if you don't care," he had said with a confident smile.

La Petite was a small but luxurious resort in St. Paul, a small village by the sea. It was a ten-minute drive from the vineyard where Catherine would be having the photo shoot and having amazing glasses of wine. The iron wrought gates pulled open as the car drove through. The windows were rolled down and she took a large handful of the cold air; she could smell the sea close by.

"Thanks," she said to the lovely driver as they pulled up in front of the main building. It was a rustic building which had large doors and windows which opened into small gardens. As the porters opened the doors from her VIP van the hotel manager and two butlers welcomed her "Bonjour Madame".

They even gave Catherine a brief history of the resort as they took a golf cart to her villa. The resort had been established in the nineties by an older couple who had come out to the sea to spend more time on themselves after all their children had grown up and gone away to start their own lives.

"They are both gone now, and the children inherited the resort. I am their eldest daughter," the woman beamed with pride. "We all run the place efficiently to uphold our parents' legacy."

The villa was a huge two-story, and it sat just next to the sea. She loved it immediately she stepped in. It had a calm décor, with a hint of rustic. The living room opened onto a balcony that led to the sea. From the doorway, she could see the calm waves of the sea.

"The bedrooms are upstairs," Maria said she was the butler that came with the villa. There were two bedrooms in the villa, one for her and the other was for Megan. Max was going to stay in a smaller cabin.

Her room was beautiful, with a great view of the sea. "Hmm…" she allowed the cool wind to blow through her long brown curls as she stood at the balcony. She had barely spent thirty minutes here and she absolutely loved it.

"There's a 24-hour butler service and meals are served at your discreet," Maria said. "If you need anything, please call me. I hope you enjoy your stay here,"

Catherine opened a complimentary bottle of wine. It was from the vineyard next door. The red wine poured into the wine glass, and she took a sniff of it, savoring the aroma.

"Amazing," she said with delight as she took a long sip. It tasted amazingly delicious. She was about to drop the empty glass when she heard Henry's voice in her head. Make use of every opportunity to promote your brand.

Rolling her eyes, she opened her camera and took pictures of the bottle of wine. As she went through the pictures, she was proud of herself. They weren't bad. It seemed her photography skills, well with her phone, were getting better. She edited them with Instagram filters and posted a couple of them, along with a selfie of her at the balcony.

After a quick nap, Catherine got into a two-piece and headed out to the sea. The resort had a private beach and at this time of the year, there were not a lot of guests around. She spotted a man in the distance, but other than him, she was alone.

She set her bag on the sand and pulled out a bottle of sunscreen from her bag. She pressed the white liquid into her hand from the tube and rubbed the cream all over her body. She laid back on the mat and pulled out a suspense novel thriller from her bag. Next to her was a glass of milkshake she had gotten from the bar of the resort.

It was beautiful and calm out here, away from the chaos of Florida. Here, the air was cooler and fresher. She loved it! The cold breeze and atmosphere engulfed her, her eyes drifting close. She could not fight it any-more, and she allowed herself to go.

It was almost dark when Catherine woke up. She was no longer alone on the beach. There was a young couple with their kids nearby who were playing in the sand. She reached for her phone which was next to her.

"Shit!" she jumped up. She had three missed calls from Megan. She must have arrived at the resort. She grabbed her bag and hurried back to the villa.

Aroma of coffee greeted her as she stepped into the cabin. Yeah, Megan was around. Her best friend was a coffee addict. She drank that stuff like fifty times a day, and nope, she wasn't exaggerating.

"Hey!" she wrapped her arms around her friend in a hug. "Sorry, I fell asleep on the beach. How was your flight?"

"Amazing. At a point I thought I would not be able to make it out of the office," Megan grimaced. She shoved a cookie which was in the complimentary basket into her mouth. "This place is amazing! Like super cool!"

"Yeah, it is," Catherine agreed.

"I am here to rest and have fun. At least I hope so. I am really hoping no one sends me any office mails," Megan grimaced.

"Did you bring your laptop?" Catherine asked.

"Yeah," Megan pouted.

Catherine rolled her eyes. Her first mistake was to bring it along. "You should have left it back in Florida."

"What if they need me to do something huh," Megan frowned.

There she went again. Her friend was such a workaholic. She took her phone from her friend's phone before Megan could stop her.

"What do you think you are doing?" Megan cried.

Catherine swiped through her apps and deleted Outlook. "Now you don't have to worry about receiving mails on the go," Catherine smiled.

Megan shook her head amused. "Fine! Now tell me you have fun activities for us tonight," Megan said.

Catherine beamed excitedly. "Yes! There's a dance tonight at the beach. Lots of wine, food, and of course company."

"An opportunity to meet men!" Megan cried.

Catherine chuckled. Like her, Megan was single. She had been married once, for about five years, but it had ended in a divorce. Megan had decided that the single life was for her. Only a few men could deal with her busy lifestyle, and unfortunately, she had not come across any. Two beautiful single women, that was them, hoping that one day love would find them. Or they would find love. Either of which came first.

After a light dinner, they changed to long matching dresses and headed out to the beach. Down the beach was a cut-out area which was well lit with small bulbs overhead. Music drifted to them as they went closer. French music, which was being danced to by a few couples. A small band sang passionately, one of them manning the mic with his sonorous voice, another playing the guitar, with the last hitting the drumsticks on the drum. They made a good team, and Catherine twirled excitedly. She giggled as Megan took her hands, and they twirled together.

After a few more steps, they headed to the bar. Megan was just going to have one glass, because she couldn't show up at her shoot drunk tomorrow. After the shoot, she could indulge as much as she wanted.

The food, however, she delved into, because it tasted so freaking good! Freshly baked bread dipped in cheese! It was yummy. And the ribs? It was totally delicious. If she wasn't careful by the time she headed back to Florida, she would have added over 10kg.

"When again is Max coming over?" Megan asked.

"Not sure yet, in a couple of days though," Catherine said. Megan wasn't much of a people's person, but from the moment she met Max, she had taken a liking to him. At a point, Catherine had thought she liked him romantically, but Megan had simply said, "He's a great guy to be around." This really said a lot because she was a good judge of character, and this made her trust Max even more. "Told him to come around sooner, so he could have some rest, but he's all work and no play. Just like you," Catherine chuckled.

Megan smiled. "You know he likes you right. And I don't mean high school kind, like he's crazy over you."

Catherine giggled. "Hell no! Max is like a... I wouldn't say older uncle, because he's like what, four or five years older. Maybe an older brother. That's all." Megan was wrong about this one. She was no child and knew when a man liked her. Max showed nothing but respect and professionalism towards her.

"If you say so," Megan said with a knowing smile. "He's cute," Megan nodded at a handsome man who was with another man who was just as handsome as he was. They were clearly checking them out, just as the women were.

"And twenty years younger," Catherine said.

Megan groaned. "You don't have to be a kill joy. But you are right, he looks young," she added, taking a longer look at them. "But the younger the berry, something the juice, right?"

Catherine laughed at her friend's sloppy attempt at reversing the saying. Megan didn't really have a type. Well, she liked mature men who didn't complain about her not having time to be all lovey.

The men moved towards them. The younger one introduced himself. "Good evening beautiful ladies. I am Antonio, and my friend here is Philippe. Can we join your company tonight?"

Catherine and Megan exchanged a look. "How old are you guys?" Megan straight-forwardly asked.

"Twenty-eight," Philippe answered for himself and his friend.

The women smiled at each other. They clearly knew they were lying, but then, they had to be at least five years younger, which was safe.

"Yes, you can," Catherine smiled.

It was an amazing night. Antonio and Philippe were investors who lived in Paris, and they were in Cannes to scout new properties for their jointly owned company. Antonio seemed way into Megan, while Philippe fancied her.

"I feel like I have seen you somewhere. You look so familiar," Phillippe said.

"She's a big-time model in the United States," Megan said.

"Aha! You are the one in the Patek advert," Philippe said.

"Yeah," Catherine smiled. She had done the ad three years ago, and it had been a huge success.

He beamed excitedly. "Tonight, just got more interesting."

At almost midnight, Catherine walked back to the cabin with Philippe with Megan and Antonio a little behind them. As much as they were here to have a vacation, and as much as the men were hot, the ladies were not inviting them over. Catherine wasn't in the mood for a one-night stand, or a vacation fling. Megan on the other hand was down for an amazing sex-filled weekend, but she had sent Catherine a text that Antonio was not her type. They would find other men they were attracted to before their holiday ended.

"I will see you tomorrow after your shoot?" Phillipe asked.

"We will see," Catherine smiled politely.

He took her hand and pressed a long kiss on it, his eyes glazed with desire as he pulled away from her. The ladies waved at the men as they walked to their cabin.

"Glad that ordeal has ended," Megan groaned as she made a cup of coffee.

"Come on, it wasn't that bad," Catherine pointed out.

Megan threw her at her. "Are you that rusty that you would take whatever crumbles thrown at you?"

Catherine giggled. "Maybe?"

"Those guys were cheesy as hell. Like they saved up all the French words in a folder to use on us. And that bullshit about them being investors? Hell no! I don't believe that" Megan said.

Catherine frowned. "They lied?"

"Definitely. Those dudes are still in college. They also lied about their ages. The only reason I let us talk to them was because I knew nothing was going to happen, I was bored, and I wanted to humor them," Megan said, opening her work laptop.

"How do you know? Philippe said—"

"Trust me, I know," Megan said confidently.

There was a ninety-five percent chance that Megan was right. She was always right. Catherine didn't know how she could always tell the truth about a person's character. Actually, she had a good sense of judgment. Catherine had lost count of how many times Megan had been right about a person was lying.

Like the time she had been sure that Catherine next door neighbor was dealing drugs. A year later, the apartment building had been surrounded by cops, and a drug lab had been discovered in his apartment. Or the time she had told Catherine that the guy she was seeing was a fraud. Catherine had been upset with her; how could the handsome wealthy man be an imposter? For about a week, she hadn't spoken to Megan, confident that she was wrong. Two months later, Catherine had become suspicious when the so-called millionaire began to ask for money to settle some bad debts. She had broken up with him shortly and a couple of weeks later, she had stumbled upon him at a restaurant with an old friend who had introduced him with a different identity. It hadn't taken a second more for her to realize he was a conman. So yes, she had come to realize that Megan was a good judge of character. Her mother's side, Megan always claimed, as some of her ancestors were gypsies. "They had the gift of intuition," Megan was fond of saying proudly.

"You are coming to the shoot with me, right?" Catherine asked.

Megan made a face that had Catherine chuckling. The first time Megan had followed her on set, she had been quite frustrated. She'd had no idea how long shots could take, and she wondered how Catherine was able to deal with the repetition that came with it.

"I love you dear, but I will pass," Megan said.

"So, what will you be doing? And don't tell me you are going to be working," Catherine rolled her eyes.

"Well, a bit of work, then I will go on the beach, and take some bomb ass pictures," Megan smiled.

"And find yourself a dashing man," Catherine added.

Megan giggled. "I will try." She took a sip of her coffee and focused her eyes on her laptop screen.

"I will be upstairs. Good night, Megan," Catherine blew a kiss at her, then darted up. The moment her head hit the pillow; she was in dreamland.

It was in the early hours of the morning when Catherine woke up. A little before four. Her room was chilly, despite the fan being turned off, and the windows barely open. Thirsty, she reached for the bedside table, and sighed, realizing she hadn't brought up a table of water. Sliding into her slippers, she headed out of the room.

She missed Devi, she thought with a smile. However, she had been unable to bring her; too many regulations and vaccines, that she had decided it was not worth it. But Devi would have had an amazing time out here on the beach.

She stopped on the stairs. She could hear Megan on the phone. Megan was still up? Her friend was way too much of a workaholic. She was pretty sure she had not gotten an eye shut since she left her.

"Hendricks needs to know about this, so we can put it on high alert. Trouble is brewing and... You couldn't sleep Cathie?"

Catherine frowned. She was still in the shadows, so how did Megan know she was there? "Who were you talking to?" Catherine asked as she stepped into the light. She grabbed a bottle of water from the pack on the table.

"My colleague," Megan smiled, her attention on her laptop.

"What are you working on that you haven't slept in like four hours?" Catherine sighed.

"If I tell you, I would have to kill you," Megan giggled, and it grew into a flew blown laughter.

Catherine rolled her eyes. "Seriously Megan? That wasn't funny."

"It was," Megan grinned.

Megan worked in the pharmaceutical industry as a consultant. Catherine had given up on understanding the chemical words her friend threw about. She had never been a science kid, sticking to the arts and humanities since she was a kid. Once, she had gone to a dinner with her friend, which she had insisted on anyway. Ten minutes in, she had been bored out. Geeky words had been tossed back and forth, and Catherine had found herself on the second bottle of champagne.

"You need to rest Megan. You are here not to work, but to have fun," Catherine chided.

"Yes ma'am. Why not go to sleep. You need all the rest you can get for morning," Megan said.

Catherine blew her a kiss then headed back upstairs. As she got to the landing upstairs, she heard Megan back on the phone again.

CHAPTER

BREAKFAST WAS AN amazing spread which was delivered by the resort's kitchen. They were seated out on the balcony, with a great view of the ocean. It was a beautiful day, with the sun straining through the clouds. Catherine knew she was on a diet, but she could not help but splurge on the croissants. They were so lovely! She munched in delight, enjoying the honey taste as it melted in her mouth.

"You eat like a wolf, one would think we don't feed you well in the US," Megan teased.

Catherine stuck her tongue at her, and continued on with her breakfast. "You sure you don't want to come with me? I don't want you to feel lonely."

"When have I ever been lonely? Don't worry, I have a lot to do. When you are done, we can go into town," Megan said, as her phone buzzed next to her.

"Your phone is ringing," Catherine pointed out.

"Yeah, it is work. I will answer it once I am powered up," Megan lifted her steaming cup of coffee. Her friend went still at a knock on the door, her eyes darting. "Expecting anyone?" she asked.

"Probably room service," Catherine said, heading back into the living room. She opened the door to see a concierge, dressed in the dark uniforms the staff of the resort wore. It was a young man, in his late teens.

"Hi, I got message for you," he said in a thick French accent, as he extended an envelope to her.

"From who?" she asked. He stared at her blankly. "Who did this come from?" she asked.

"For you," he responded.

He clearly did not understand what she meant, she realized. "Thanks," she began to say as he hurried off. She opened the envelope and pulled out a note. It was from the winery, bearing the logo. It read:

Hi Catherine,

*Let's meet in five minutes at Le Blu Café
in town for a brief meeting about the shoot.*

Ernesto

Catherine rolled her eyes. What happened to a text? Or even a call? She headed back into the cabin to see Megan watching her.

"Who was that?" Megan asked.

"A concierge. He came with a note from the winery. I have to meet them at a nearby café. Don't miss me," Catherine smiled.

Megan gave her the middle finger, and she giggled as she headed upstairs to change from her lingerie. She slipped into a green flowery long dress, which she would eventually change from during the shoot. Her face was bare, well except for a slash of moisturizer and sunscreen which she knew would soon come off once she was seated in front of the makeup artist.

"Have fun!" Megan called her as she headed out of the cabin.

"You too! And go out!" Catherine waved back. However, she was pretty sure she would find Megan in front of her laptop when she returned, with a fresh cup of coffee. That girl needed a real break from work. She worked way too hard. When the shoot was over, she was going to dedicate more time to her friend. Hide her laptop or something but just get her out of the house.

The resort had gotten a taxi for her, and it was waiting out front. The driver was a slender older man, with grey hair. He looked really good for his age, sixty-two, and he was proud to show her pictures of his grandchildren, two of whom were in America.

"No, I don't know them," Catherine smiled, handing back the photographs of his grandchildren in the United States.

He droned on and on about his family while she took in the view of the small town before them. It was beautiful, with old cobblestone houses that gave her a feel like she was on a movie set. Perhaps one day, she would relocate to the countryside, in a different country in Europe, or somewhere in South America. She would have a farm, where she would rear hens, and play around with Devi. Yeah, that seemed like a cool life to resign herself to.

"Here we go," the driver said as he pulled in front of a café.

It was a quaint café, with chairs and tables outside. It was still early in the day, so there were no patrons.

She paid him and headed into the café. The aroma of hot bread still in the oven greeted her, and she sighed. She'd had enough breakfast, she could not afford to eat more, right?

"Bonjour!" an excited man greeted her from behind the counter.

"Bonjour!" she smiled back at him, as she settled down to a table. There was no menu, but she had seen a chalkboard at the entrance listing the breakfast choices for the day.

"What will you have?" the man asked in English, coming over to her.

"How did you know I wasn't French?" Catherine lifted a brow.

A broad smile spread on his face. "Your accent. It is American," the man answered.

Fair enough. She looked American. Whatever traces of Spanish she had in her family had been lost generations ago. "I will have a cup of coffee. I am meeting with a couple of others. Has anyone come here from the winery?" Catherine asked, looking around, but she was the only patron around.

"No, you the only one who come here. First person today, so you get free coffee," the man smiled.

Catherine flashed a smile at him. That was weird. The meeting was supposed to be by eight, and she was ten minutes late.

The coffee tasted amazingly nice. If not divine. She had to get some of this brew on her way back to Florida. She went through her social media accounts as she waited. There was so much going on out there that she could not keep up. Henry wanted her to join Tik-Tok and make some dance videos. Hell no! She was a terrible dancer, besides she would look so silly.

"You sure you don't want bread to go with that?" the older man asked as he refilled her cup.

She sighed as she looked at her watch. She had been waiting for about twenty minutes now. "Let me get back to you on that," she flashed a smile at him. She didn't want to have another breakfast and be bloated during the shoot. That would affect her productivity. Where were they? It was a horrible thing to keep her waiting. She dialed Max's number again, but it was still unreachable.

Ah! She had almost forgotten that she had the number of one of the people from the winery. Ernesto was his name right? He was the one who had sent her the note. She scrolled through her phone for his number, groaning in the process. She had a terrible habit of not saving numbers. Annoying, actually, but she liked the chaos of trying to figure out through her call log who was who, and beaming with victory when she actually called the right person.

She got through two calls with the wrong persons, before she got through to Ernesto. Yeah, she needed to change that attitude.

"Bonjour Ernesto. This is Catherine," Catherine introduced herself.

"Catherine!" he sang with excitement. "I hope you had a great night!"

"Yes, yes. Where are you please? I have been waiting for you guys at Le Bleu," she said, looking around.

"I don't understand," Ernesto said, sounding confused.

Catherine frowned. "A message was delivered this morning that we have a meeting here, at the café," Catherine explained.

"No, no. We sent no message. We meet at the winery at noon, I would have called if there was a change of time, I have your number," Ernesto said.

"Umm… okay." Catherine picked up the note, staring at it confused. It was addressed to her and had the winery's logo. What sort of prank was this? Or had it been sent to her mistakenly?

"Having that breakfast?" the older man asked with an eager smile.

"Yes please," Catherine said. She was going to wait a few minutes more. Perhaps there was some sort of miscommunication because it just didn't make any sense, that someone would set out to deceive her.

Twenty minutes later, Catherine was headed back to the resort. She had watched and waited as the café filled up for breakfast, but no one from the winery had met with her. She dialed Max's number. Perhaps he had left her the message, but it was still unreachable. Now, she was upset. Who would do such a silly thing? And why? It really didn't add up. She was going to insist on an explanation when she went for the shoot. She still had about three hours left, so she would enjoy the rest of her morning at the beach.

"You won't believe what happened!" Catherine called out as she walked in through the front door. She was surprised not to see Megan working at the table.

"Megan?" she called, heading out to the balcony. There was no one there. She had probably gone for a walk on the beach, Catherine began to think. But why did she think otherwise?

She looked around the living room. It was eerily quiet, except for one thing. Her heart was racing in excitement. She found herself racing up the stairs to Megan's room.

"Oh God!" she cried out at the doorway of her friend's room. It was like a tornado had gone through the room. Megan's clothes, bags and shoes had been scattered all over. The bed had been upturned and the shelves of the wardrobe flung open. The pillows were ripped from their pillowcases and tossed about.

"Megan!" she called as she bolted out to the room's balcony, almost stumbling over Megan's shoe.

She ran to her bedroom, going still at the peace and calm that greeted her. It was untouched, a contrast to the room she had just left. Her heart raced faster as she stepped into her room. She quickly grabbed her phone and dialed Megan's number. It was ringing, not just in her ear, but also right there in the house.

She quietly, on tiptoes returned to Megan's room. She could hear the phone ringing from somewhere. Her ears carefully traced it, and she pulled it from under Megan's black coat. The color drained from Catherine's face. Where was Megan?

CHAPTER 6

CATHERINE'S HANDS SHOOK as she took a long gulp from the bottle. She stood on the balcony, and on a normal day, she would be captivated by the view, but not today. Not when her friend was missing, with her room torn apart.

"Mademoiselle."

She turned to the chubby police constable who had joined her on the balcony. He had a round stomach and a heavy moustache. She had run to the reception and breathlessly told them to call the police. In about ten minutes they had arrived, and she had poured out to them that her friend Megan was missing, with her room vandalized.

"Please tell me you know who took her," Catherine said.

"Madam, we found nothing," the constable said.

Catherine frowned. "What do you mean you found nothing? Her room was ripped apart! I don't know where Megan is! She would go nowhere without her phone!" Catherine cried out.

The constable sighed, patting a green handkerchief over his sweaty face. The room was cold, and she wondered why he was covered in sweat.

"Your friend is fine. There is no blood. No struggle. Your friend will come back soon," the constable said.

Catherine glared at him. "No struggle? Have you seen her room?" she pointed out. That was enough proof that something terrible had happened.

"She might have done it herself. You Americans are funny, need attention," he added with a shrug.

Catherine stared at him in disbelief. Clearly, she had not heard him right "Megan would never do such a thing!" Her friend was responsible with no time for shenanigans. She played by the rules, and would not carry out such a mischievous act.

A young officer hurried towards them. He whispered into the ears of the older man who sighed, as he dabbed the handkerchief over his forehead.

"What is it?" Catherine asked.

"No CCTV to see who came into the cabin," the constable said.

"What!" Catherine cried. "But there are cameras everywhere."

"Fake cameras. Only the one in the reception works. Village is safe. Private. No incident, not even a theft in over ten years. This is the first incident," the constable said, looking at her pointedly.

Catherine wanted to stomp her feet in rage. How dare he try to insinuate that what had happened was their fault? "You need to find my friend. I know she is in danger."

"I am sure your friend went for a walk on the beach. Or she needs some time alone. Or maybe she meets a fine man. We have plenty of them here," the constable flashed his large teeth at her.

He pulled out a squeezed pack of cards which had stains, and handed her one from the deck. "Call me if she is not back by evening," he said.

She watched them go with dread. She could not believe it. They were actually not going to do anything. Seriously! She headed upstairs and stood in the doorway, staring at the room. The officers had tried to make the room neat, but it still looked out of place. Something had happened here that involved her friend, and she was deeply worried.

Her phone buzzed, making her jump. It was Max calling. "Max where have you been!" she yelled.

"Is everything okay?" Max asked.

"Megan is missing, and the police are doing nothing about it!" Catherine cried.

Silence, and then… "What do you mean Megan is missing?"

"I went to this café and when I got back, her room was ransacked and she's nowhere to be found," Catherine explained.

"Maybe she went for a walk or something," Max suggested.

"Leaving behind her phone? And a ransacked room? Not Megan," Catherine refused.

"Have you spoken to the police?" Max asked.

"They are impossible. They think Megan ran off, but she's not twenty and in love. I believe she has been kidnapped by the person who ransacked the room. We need to find her Max," Catherine said. She knew nothing about kidnapped victims, but she knew every second that passed was critical to saving her friend's life.

"I think you should be patient Catherine. Maybe the police is right. The resort is a safe place, and so is the town. She probably went into town to get something and will be back soon. And I am sure there's an explanation for the ransacked room huh? If she isn't back by nighttime, then we can have a reason to be worried," Max suggested.

"Megan will never do such a thing," Catherine insisted.

"If she's not back by evening, I promise you we will do something about it. But for now, I need you to relax and get ready for your shoot," Max said.

Her shoot! She had completely forgotten about it. She was supposed to be at the winery by now. "I don't think I can do it. Not with all this uncertainty," Catherine admitted. How could she smile for the cameras when she had no idea what had happened to her friend?

"They will be displeased if we ask them to reschedule. They have spent a huge amount of time and money for this production," Max said.

Catherine sighed. She knew he was right. Flying her into France, and booking the cabin for her, as well as her professional fees. It was indeed a huge commitment, but how could she concentrate and act like all was fine, when it wasn't?

"I have to go Max, I will keep you updated," Catherine said with resignation.

Ten minutes later, she was on her way to the winery. Something bothered her; it had been bothering her since, but it was not until the cab pulled up to the front gate of the winery that it hit her. The note! Someone had sent her that note to get her out of the way to the cafe, where she had waited for almost an hour. At the time she had found it odd why a wrong message would be delivered to her. But it now made sense. Whoever had sent that note had wanted her out of the way.

"Oh dear!" she cried as she went pale, her hands shaking in fright. The note had been a lure to get her from the cabin, so Megan could be taken away. This meant something that terrified her even more; whoever it was knew her well enough to know the reason she was in Cannes.

On a normal day, Catherine would be having an awesome time. Amazing wine. Great scenery, and a photographer who was hot and gorgeous, with a great sense of humor. But not today. As she swirled the glass of wine, she realized that she should have postponed the shoot instead, because the last thing on her mind was the ad. All she could think of was Megan. Where was she? Who had taken her?

What if she had been kidnapped by a sex-trafficking gang? But didn't they usually go for younger girls? Megan would make a terrible sex slave. She would yell out cuss words that would make even a sailor blush at whatever customer had purchased her. The thought of it made her giggle.

"Oh yes! I love that smile!" Gail the photographer said, pulling her back to reality for an instant.

Or what if she had been taken as part of an organ harvesting scheme? This made her get cold. She was terrified by the image of her friend placed on cold steel while her heart and kidneys were being removed by a masked doctor.

"That's a fierce look! I want more of that!" the photographer called.

Two hours later, Catherine was more than grateful to be done with the shoot. It had been horrendous with her thoughts far away as she worried about Megan. She hurried over to her phone and pulled it out. There were no calls from Megan or anyone else.

"Are you sure no one sent a note to the resort?" Catherine asked Ernesto.

He smiled at her, and she wondered why he wasn't frustrated as this had to be the hundredth time, she had asked this very question.

"No mademoiselle. We would call if we wanted to convey any message to you," Ernesto said.

She groaned. How could she have been so naïve? She was in a little town in Cannes not in the nineteenth century, she should have known better that she was being led into a ruse. Right? But how was she supposed to know that this would happen?

"I hope you are okay Megan. Please," Catherine whispered with a heavy heart.

Catherine returned to the resort with a long look. She headed to the front desk with Maria quickly apologizing to her.

"We so sorry about what happened. Never has such happened here at the resort. Never!" Maria quickly said.

"A staff brought a note this morning. Young, brown hair, with freckles," Catherine said.

"Dominic. He just graduated secondary school and helps here at the resort. He's a good boy. He will not vandalize your room," Maria defended.

She didn't know about that, but he had to know who had caused the damage and taken Megan. "I want to talk to him. He knows something."

Maria frowned, clearly not pleased with the accusation. "He left in the afternoon. A call from his mother.

He will be back tomorrow morning. But I tell you, he's a good boy. He knows nothing."

That was not for Maria to decide. "I was told there are no CCTVs of the resorts," Catherine said with a pointed look at Maria who quickly looked away. She had not been worried about security, assured that nothing would happen out here, but for the CCTVs to be dummies? That was terrible!

"They cost too much. And nothing bad happens here until you come along," Maria mumbled.

"There were two men, Phillippe and Antonio, guests staying here. We danced and talked yesterday. Are they still around?" Catherine had told the police about the men. They were the only ones they had been within close contact yesterday. What if they and the courier was part of a syndicate who robbed foreigners. What if Megan had recognized one of them and they had taken her? Or worse?

"I cannot give information about our guests to you," Maria said firmly.

Catherine held her gaze, and Maria remained unmoved. If only she had been this firm in following the right process, none of this would be happening.

Catherine headed back to the resort, and found herself looking over her shoulder. She was wary and uncomfortable with her surroundings. Yesterday she had thought this place was paradise-like, but now she was eager to leave. But she couldn't, at least not yet. She wanted to be here when Megan returned.

She stood at the doorway of the living room, just looking in. There was a dark presence looming in the cabin that she could not describe. One that made her convinced that Megan was in danger. All she had wanted was for them to have a good time away from the chaos of Florida, and now her best friend was missing.

"You are going to come home," Catherine said aloud with conviction.

As much as she wanted to be indoors that evening, Catherine headed outside to the beach. The music did nothing to her as she joined the other guests. With relief, she spotted Antonio and Phillippe. They were chatting with younger girls. She headed straight to them.

"Hi, can I have a moment with you two?" she said stepping aside.

"We heard about a theft at your cabin. Hope you are okay," Philippe said, putting an arm on her shoulder.

She looked into his eyes, trying to figure out if he was pretending. But damn, she couldn't tell.

"Umm… yeah. I want to ask, did either of you see Megan today?" she asked.

"No, we didn't. We looked forward to seeing both of you tonight," Antonio said.

Yeah right, and she had seen them flirting with other women. "Are you sure about that?" she pushed.

The men exchanged a look. "No, we have nothing to do with the theft if that's what you are insinuating," Antonio said firmly.

"I did not say that. But you lied to me and my friend about you guys being businessmen. So, what else can you both be lying about?" Catherine asked fiercely.

Philippe gulped. "How… How did you know we are not businessmen?"

Once again Megan was right! That gypsy blood was something right? "How is not your business. But maybe you decided to kidnap her because she figured out you were students and playing mindless games huh?

Antonio looked around, hoping the women were not close. "We had no idea your friend was kidnapped until now. All we wanted was a good time with two beautiful women. It is not a crime to lie, everyone does it. Look, we want no trouble. We just want to have a good time," Antonio defended.

"We hope you find your friend," Phillippe said, as Antonio dragged him back to the women.

It did seem like a silly reason for them to go after Megan. They were just college students trying to have a wild weekend. She looked around, taking in the smiles and laughter, and it made her feel choked up. She turned around, stumbling over as she headed back to the cabin.

That night, she could not sleep. She lay in bed, the light turned on, with a chair against the door. The windows were closed, with the fan on. She kept drifting in and out of sleep; the slightest noise made her wake, and reach for the knife under her pillow. She had gotten it from the kitchenette. It was a bread knife, but if she found herself in a dire situation, she would stab it so hard, it would destabilize her assailant.

The nightmares also kept her awake. They were incoherent, but she knew they involved Megan, making her worry every time she awoke.

She got out of bed at five in the morning, unable to keep up with the pretense of trying to get some sleep. Despite her will, she found herself in Megan's room. She stood in the middle, staring around for nothing. Perhaps something that would give her a hint of what had happened. Her eyes finally rested on Megan's purse. Inside was Megan's international passport and some dollar bills. She frowned at this. Why had the vandalizers not taken them? They had raided the room for money, right?

It also brought back the question, why Megan and not her? After finding the state of the room, she had checked her bag for her money and jewelries, and they had all been there. And now the same with Megan? If there was anyone to steal from or even kidnap, it was her, Catherine. Megan was not a celebrity, neither did she come off as flashy; she wasn't poor either, but she was modest. Catherine was the one who wore diamonds; the one with potential net worth.

With none of their valuables gone, she could not help but worry about what was happening. Had Megan been at the wrong place at the wrong time? Had the kidnap been meant for her instead? But why send her away from the cabin? Had it been intended that she would be kidnapped when she returned home? But it was no secret that she was not alone in the cabin. They had been out together all night and were even registered at the front desk as guests. None of this made sense. Every line of thought only made her more confused.

Her phone rang. It was Ernesto calling. Today, they were supposed to continue with the shoot. As much as she wanted to tell him to cancel, she had signed a contract, and needed to go through with it.

CATHERINE MADE A stop at the police station which was a small building perched in a corner of the village. The aroma of coffee drifted to her, and she felt nausea rise. She had tried to take a cup of herself, but it had only reminded her of Megan.

"I want to speak to the constable," she said to an officer she remembered from the day before.

He directed her to an office. Inside was the constable, having a large breakfast. He frowned at the sight of her.

"Good morning. I believe you have gotten in touch with your friend. Yes?" he said, shoving a croissant into his mouth.

"No. Megan hasn't called. She hasn't sent a message either. I went through her things this morning. Her passport, jewelries and money were all in her bag. She would not leave without them. And why did the thieves not take anything?" Catherine asked.

"Your friend? Has she done something like this before? Leave for days without contact?" the man asked.

"Well…" Due to her job, Megan was always on the move, that Catherine had termed her flight risk as a joke. She was always going on impromptu trips for her company to different places around the world. Despite her being a world-class model, Megan had travelled more than she had. Weeks could go by, and she would be unable to reach her, only for her to return that she had jetted off for a retreat.

"This is different," Catherine defended.

"Your answer tells me different," the constable said.

"Megan would not just suddenly up and leave when we were on a vacation. Without her passport? Leaving behind her phone? And with her room ransacked? That's not her. I am telling you she was kidnapped. Explain this!" she shoved the note at the chief who flipped it over. "The winery denied sending this over. Someone used this as a rouse to get me out of the cabin. You must interview the courier that brought it over. Everyone! I am convinced Megan's life is in danger."

"As you can see, we are short-staffed. We do not have the resources to find some crazy rich girl who is pulling this stunt for attention," the constable said.

Catherine was pissed. Megan would never do something this crazy. Never! She loathed attention. She was barely on social media, and the Instagram account she had was private, with only access to a few close friends. She lived a private life, and respected that privacy.

The constable's eyes widened as Catherine dumped a wad of cash on the table. "You don't have the resources. Well use this and find my friend! If anything happens to her, you will be held responsible, and will have to explain to the American government why you did nothing to protect her citizen!" Catherine yelled.

His eyes widened at her threat. "We will investigate right away," he said, shamelessly reaching for the money. She shook her head in disgust as she spun out of the office to her waiting cab.

The rest of the shoot was an ordeal, and she was more than glad when it was wrapped up for the day. One more day, and it was going to be over.

"We are having lunch in the garden," Ernesto said with a smile. As much as she wanted to be alone in her own thoughts, she didn't want to be impolite. She headed with him to the garden where the production cast were already eating. He patted a chair next to him and she sat.

She reached for her phone in her bag, and her hand came out with a phone and a note that made her frown. The bag she had taken with her was a different bag from yesterday. She had given it to Megan to take to the beach on the night of the party. She had absently taken it from Megan's room back to hers after the ransack. She frowned at the note. Written on it was "I still love you" in dark ink. Her frown deepened as she tried to figure out if it was the same writing with the note at the hotel.

Below the profession of love was an address: Magic Café.

Her heart caught, and she feared it was going to explode. This was not an old note from back home Someone had given the note to Megan here in Cannes. Certainly not herself, because she would bloody well remember. So, when had Megan gotten this note? Ever since Megan arrived, they had been at each other's side. The only time they were not together had been when she went to the café after receiving the note. This meant one thing, the note had gotten to Megan sometime after she arrived in Cannes. That was the only explanation that made sense.

Who had written her this note? Did Megan have a lover who had followed her to Cannes? Was the constable somehow right, and Megan was cuddled with her lover while she panicked over her. She shook her head; Megan was no nun. She was quite vocal about her sex and romance life. The time she had been dating a married man, she had confided in her. Just as she had done with that retired senator. Megan knew that she would never judge her, neither would she spill her secrets to anyone.

"Where is this?" Catherine showed the paper to Ernesto.

He grinned at the first line. "Meeting up with a lover?"

"Umm… something like that," Catherine said.

"It is about twenty minutes from the winery. Close to the outskirts of town. It is not hard to miss, I could take you there," he said with excitement.

"Thanks Ernesto, but I will get a taxi," she said as she hurried up, barely touching her meal.

Magic was a small coffee shop, even smaller than La Bleu, with a small space inside, and with few patrons outside. It was about a few minutes' walk from the resort Catherine realized. She headed straight for the counter which was attended by a pretty girl in her twenties. The girl's eyes widened in admiration at the sight of Catherine. She did not know who she was, but just coming from a shoot, with just a change of outfit, Catherine looked like no ordinary tourist.

"Bonsoir, what will you like to order?" the girl asked, with a broad smile as she stood straight.

"Nothing yet. Where you here yesterday?" Catherine asked.

"Yes," the girl nodded.

Catherine showed the girl a picture of Megan. It was one of the few ones she had of her friend who was camera shy. She used to say, "I am not photogenic, so why bother?"

"Did you see her yesterday? Or the day before, or even today? It is very important. Please remember," Catherine said.

The girl looked closely at the picture and nodded, making Catherine excited.

"She was here yesterday. She had on a Fendi coat, last summer," the girl said.

Yes! It was her! She had gotten Megan that coat last year's Christmas. "That's her! When was this? Was she here with someone?

"She was here around seven. I know this because we were still making the first pot of coffee," the girl said.

Which was about a few minutes after she had left the resort, she figured out.

"Was she here with someone?" Catherine repeated.

"Yes. A man," the girl said.

Catherine's eyes widened. "A man? Who was he? Can you describe him? Please I need to know everything you can remember!"

The girl took a worried step back, and Catherine realized how crazy she must be asking these questions. She took a deep breath and said calmly, "I am sorry. The woman in this picture is my friend and she's missing."

The girl's eyes went soft. "I am so sorry, but I don't remember much. Customers were coming in, and things became crazy. They only ordered coffee and I didn't take much notice of him because I had to attend to other customers. All I know is that he was tall, with a beard, and American. I could tell from the accent," she added with a smile.

"And where did they go? When did they leave?"

The girl shook her sadly. "They didn't stay long. Barely even touched their coffee. Just kept money on the table and left. Next, I looked over, they were leaving. Sorry, but I don't know where they went to. That's all I know."

"Do you have CCTVs?" Even before she asked, she already knew what the response would be.

"No, we don't," the girl said.

"Thank you," Catherine said. The information she had gotten, despite not being detailed, was valuable. The girl's eyes lit up as she slid some dollar notes to her. She quickly looked around, before tucking it into her apron.

As Catherine headed out of the coffee shop, her phone rang. It was Max.

"Have you heard from Megan?" he asked.

"No, I just left a coffee shop where she met some strange dude yesterday morning. I am very sure he has something to do with all of this," Catherine said.

"Cathie, don't get yourself involved in this," Max said.

What did he mean, she frowned. "Megan is my best friend and you expect me to act like everything is fine when she's missing? Really Max?" Catherine snapped.

"My apologies, but the police are currently investigating. You should leave them to do their job," Max said.

"How did you know the police are involved?" Catherine asked with a frown.

"Because I am in Cannes? At the police station? Let's meet at the cabin in five minutes," Max said.

Her shoulders relaxed with calm as the call ended. She was glad that Max was around and was looking for Megan as well. He was that way, taking charge of things.

There was a knock on the door and Catherine dropped her wine glass. She was on her second glass as she waited for Max. Grabbing a knife, she advanced to the door, and looked through the peephole. It was Max.

She opened the door and threw her arms around him. She had never been more grateful to see him than now. And he smelled so good as always.

"One would think you haven't seen me in months," Max teased as he pulled the knife from her grip. "What were you going to do with this?" he asked with humor.

"Hurt someone if someone attacked me at the door?" she shrugged as she returned to the counter.

"And what about the self-defense classes?" he asked, lifting a brow.

Years ago, he had made her take self-defense classes, with Megan's encouragement, and every year he ensured she went back for a refreshment. But she doubted that would do much if she was being attacked by a heavily built man, who was three times her size.

"I am so glad you are here," she said with all honesty as she stared at him. It was a relief to have someone she could trust around, someone she could count on, and who understood well enough not to think that Megan would run off, without any notice.

"Had to end my Dubai trip to be here," he said, shrugging out of his jacket. When had he gotten so buff? She wondered. And that tan? She had no idea that Dubai was that hot. She pulled away from her thoughts, rebuffing herself for even admiring him for a moment.

"What did the police tell you?" Catherine asked as he folded his arms around his chest, her eyes following that move as she chided herself again. What had gotten into her? She could only blame Megan for putting such thoughts in her head.

"They have found nothing. They still think Megan needed a break and is with a lover or just wants to be alone," Max said.

"I found this in my bag this morning," Catherine slid the note across the counter to him.

He frowned at the paper. "In your bag? Have you let anyone in since yesterday?" he asked tensely, going over to the back door to examine the lock.

"I gave the bag to Megan the night she came around. She didn't bring a small purse and needed one to put her phone. I retrieved it from her room, and it must have been in there," she said.

Her explanation didn't seem to calm him as he stepped onto the balcony. She had no idea what he was poking around for, but when he returned, he locked the door. "They lied on their website. They have a lousy security system here," he said, clearly not pleased.

"I must show this to the police. If they find the man, they will find Megan," Catherine said with conviction.

"I don't want you involved in any of this," Max said, as he pulled closer to her, placing his hands on her shoulders.

God! Why did he have to smell so good? "Did you change your perfume?" she asked before she could stop herself.

Max was stunned at her question. Then he chuckled. "Yes, it is an oud scent. Decided to give it a try. You like it?" he asked, holding her gaze.

Oh God! Was she blushing? "It's… it's not bad. As I was saying Max, it's been almost forty-eight hours since Megan went missing. I have no idea what's going on, but something sinister is. I can feel it," Catherine said.

His phone buzzed and he pulled it out of his pocket to answer. "Hello, yes constable, this is Max," Max said. Catherine tensed up at the mention of the constable's name. "Yes. She's here with me. I don't think that's appropriate. A picture is better."

Catherine growled at the one-sided conversation. What were the on about?

He looked at his Rolex. "Ten minutes I suppose."

"What did he want?" Catherine asked immediately the call was over. She went still as Max's cold eyes rested on her.

"They want you to identify a body."

THE RIDE TO the station was probably the longest journey when in actual fact it was about ten minutes. Catherine's heart beat fast as she clenched her fingers. Max had not told her much; only that the cops had found a body and wanted her to identify it. He had refused them going to a morgue, insisting that pictures of the body be taken.

"Hey, it is going to be okay," Max said, as he pulled the truck he had rented into the vacant spot in front of the station. He placed his hand over her, and for a minute it was assuring.

The atmosphere in the station was tense as they walked in, different from earlier in the morning. She could feel the gloom resting over, with eyes on them as they walked over to the constable's office. That afternoon, he was nursing a glass of whiskey. He offered them a glass, and they both shook their head, turning him down.

"What do you have for us?" Max said as he settled into the chair, his eyes and face firm, Catherine could not help but think that he was suited for this sort of thing, whatever it was.

"We found a body in the woods, close to the out-skirts of town. Not too far from the resort," the constable said.

Catherine gasped, her hand flying to her mouth.

"Kids who went there to fool around stumbled across it, and reported it in. Drastic business I tell you. We have not had a murder in over twenty years and that was done by poor Regina in self-defense," the constable said with a sigh.

"Is it Megan?" Catherine whispered.

"It was a kid. Dominic. One of us," the constable shook his head.

Catherine's heart calmed down, at least for a moment. It wasn't Megan! It wasn't her! Oh God! Megan was still alive. She had to be! And then… "Dominic? Is that the kid from the resort? The one who gave me the note?"

The constable nodded. "Yes. We went to his house this morning after you were here." He coughed, with a quick look at Max, and then at her, as if pleading with her not to tell him all that had happened earlier in the day. "His grandma. She lives with him. She hadn't seen him since yesterday. Thought he was with his cousins."

He reached for a file and pulled out a photograph. He gave a look at Max who nodded before he placed it in front of Catherine.

She winced as she stared at the dead kid. Yes, that was him, the courier guy. His eyes were wide open in death, as he stared into the unknown. His neck was scarred red as if… Max took the picture from her.

"He was strangled," Max said.

The constable didn't seem surprised by Max's knowledge, but Catherine was. "Strangled?" she whispered.

"Yes. From behind, but the autopsy would have to confirm that. No sign of any weapons around. His phone was missing, but his wallet intact with his IDs, I suppose he was killed sometime yesterday afternoon, but also again, the autopsy would confirm that," the constable said.

"It was him. He was the one who gave me the note… I… Do you know who did this to him?" Megan asked. The poor kid didn't deserve to die. He had done nothing wrong.

"We are still trying to find out who did this. Dominic was one of us. A hardworking kid. Went to school with my daughter. Was working to save money for college you know. Worked hard. We need you to find out who did this," the constable said, with a pointed look at her.

She wanted to retort that now he needed her help, when in the past she had pleaded before he could help her, but a calming look from Max made her decide otherwise. "I really don't know much. Around seven yesterday morning, he came to the door with a note. He told me it was urgent from the hotel and that he had booked a cab which was waiting for me. That's all the interaction I had with him," Catherine said.

"My men have been to the winery. No one there sent the note," the constable said. "Tell me where you were all through yesterday."

"You have got to be kidding!" Catherine gave him an incredulous look. Was he somehow insinuating that she had something to do with Dominic's death and Megan's kidnap.

"He knows you did nothing, it is just for formality's sake," Max assured her, with a calm smile.

She took a deep breath and relayed the events of the past day while the constable scribbled on a note pad.

When she was done, she took another deep breath. The past twenty-four hours had been quite eventful.

"We will look into this to check it all backs up," the constable said.

"So, what does all of this means?" Catherine thought aloud.

"We are not sure, but Dominic probably recruited to deliver that note to you, and was killed to cover the tracks of the person who took your friend. It is just a theory, but I think that's what happened," the constable said. "Rest assured, we are going to find out who did this and upset the peace of our town."

"And my friend? If this man can kill a child, he can do worse to Megan," Catherine said, quickly telling him of the man Megan had met in the café.

"We will find your friend," the constable said. However, he didn't sound sure of himself.

"We should never have come here," Catherine said. She was seated at the counter, back in the resort with Max who was eating dinner brought over by the restaurant.

"You are not responsible for this Catherine," he said.

"We could have had some fun back in Florida. All I wanted was to give her a good time. That's all

I wanted," Catherine said shakily as tears welled in her eyes.

"Hey, it's okay. It's going to be fine," Max said as he reached for her. He pulled her into his arms, and she melted against his body. He felt so warm, and she felt safe. Had he always felt this way she wondered.

His phone buzzed and he pulled away to read a message. She wondered if it was from his girlfriend. Did he have one? He knew he had been dating a lawyer a couple of months ago, but he hadn't brought her up in the past week. "So, the shoot ends tomorrow," he said.

She nodded in agreement. This was her least enjoyable shoot for obvious reasons.

"I have another gig lined up in Singapore. It starts in two days. They need you to headline a gala at Marina Bay and we have an ad for a hotel opening."

"You really are serious Max? You expect me to leave Cannes to go to Singapore? To act like everything is all right? Hell no!" she said fiercely, her arms folded around her chest. Was it her imagination or did his gaze drop to her boobs? God! Once this ordeal was over, she had to get laid badly.

"I know Megan is your best friend, but you can't put your life on hold for her. So many opportunities are springing up right now and you need to go for them," Max said.

"I am not leaving Cannes until we find Megan," she said stubbornly. Screw all the jobs in the world! She cared for nothing for them. All that mattered right now was Megan's safe return.

"Okay, tell me. What exactly are you going to be doing here? Helping the cops investigate?" he asked sarcastically.

She shot him a dirty look. "If I have to."

"You do know that intervening in an investigation could get you locked up?" he asked. "There's nothing you can do here but wait, and get hurt," he added.

"What do you mean?" she asked with a frown.

"We have a killer out there, who probably took Megan, and you are snooping around. What if he comes after you?" Max asked.

Catherine gulped. "He… Why would he do that?" she asked.

Max shrugged. "I don't know. I am not a killer. But staying in Cannes puts you at security risk. I can't be around to look after you all the time, and the cops are short-staffed, they can't do the same. In Singapore, you will be safe from all this drama. The chief will keep us updated, let us know when they find Megan."

"And if they don't?" Catherine whispered her deepest fear, as tears pooled in her eyes. What if Megan was never found? She had read news articles where people solicited news of their loved ones, even ten years later.

"We are going to find her. I promise you," Max reassured her as he swiped a tear that rolled down her cheek.

She pulled away from him, sniffing back the rest of the tears. "I'm sorry… I just… All of this is draining," she said.

He nodded in understanding.

"I… I need to think about this over the night. About leaving Cannes," Catherine said as she moved past him up the stairs.

That night, she laid in bed without fear of someone coming in to assault her. Her door was only locked, with her window open. Well, this was after Max had checked her room twice since they returned, as well as the rest of the other house. She found his bravery charming, but what would he do if they were attacked? He didn't seem like the kind of guy who would fight back, but then he wouldn't abandon her either.

She rolled over on the bed with a sigh. She knew Max was right. Her stay here was no good. She didn't know the town well enough to go in search of Megan.

Besides, there was the language barrier, which would limit her from communicating properly. But she didn't want to leave the village. She wanted to be there when Megan was found and brought back in one piece. Being away, going to Singapore, and then back home was like she had given up, like she didn't care. But being here was no better; she would just be more frustrated every day that passed by.

She reached for her phone and dialed Megan's number. Her heart raced in excitement with the hope that the call would be picked, and she would hear Megan's voice. That her friend would tell her, "Got you! I am stuck up in a hotel with my mysterious lover!" But all she got was the service operator informing her that the number she tried to reach was unavailable.

She pulled up a picture of Megan and stared at it tenderly. "I hope you are fine my dear friend. I really hope so," she said pleadingly.

Max watched in the dark as the lazy police officers went about looking for Megan, and finding who killed the kid. Their attempts were futile. They held no torch to qualify them to even have a hint of who he was. He could be right in their midst, and they wouldn't be able to identify him as the killer. But Max, now that was one to be careful about. Extremely careful of. He was no fool. Pretty smart with experience, and that was why he was living and watching in the shadows, staying away from all prying eyes.

"Can I get you anything else?" the cahier asked.

He shook his head as he got the snacks he had just purchased. He was going to be living off these for a while, with the realization that eating in public put him at risk at being questioned or suspicious by the locals.

He drove halfway to the woods, then parked at a local car park, before making his way by foot through a path lest frequented by the locals. It let to a small clearing site, where an abandoned factory sat.

He grinned as he sensed her fear as he walked into the dark room. Bruises covered her lips, and her hands.

"How have you been? Enjoying the solitude?" he mocked.

"Fucking bastard! You are going to pay, I promise you!" she snapped at him when he removed a tape from her mouth.

"Just like you are paying for your past actions? That day will never come for me. I will live till I am old and grey. Probably die in my sleep. Can't say the same for you," he teased.

"Bastard!" she threw at him.

"Where is it Megan? Where is it?" he asked. "Tell me and I will probably let you go."

The bitch laughed, pissing him even more. She was mocking him. She had done so when she had the upper hand, and she was doing same, despite knowing that she was under his control, in his terrain.

He struck her across the face. He frowned, clenching his fist, as her laughter grew harder. He hated her. He fucking hated her!

"You are such a loser. You better kill me now, because I am never telling you where it is," she smiled.

He grabbed a plier. Grabbing her hand, he plucked off a finger nail. She let out a muffled scream. And then burst into another bout of laughter.

He smashed the plier against her face. Over and over he did as it bruised her face. Yet, the bitch kept on laughing.

"Guess you won't keep laughing when I do same to your little friend huh?" he threatened. That made her go silent.

"You dare not do anything to Catherine!" she growled, struggling against her restrains.

It was his time to laugh. "Why not? I am going to scar that beautiful face of hers. Cut off those legs so she can never use them. I won't kill her, just make her suffer," he threatened. "But I don't have to do all of that, if you just tell me where it is," he added softly.

She looked up at him with cold-blooded eyes. "I am never telling you," she said firmly.

He struck her again, and this time around, he didn't stop until his fists were bloodied through the black gloves he had on. "I am going to give you some time to think things over. When I get back, I want answers," he said as he opened a case. Inside were long knives, newly sharpened for clarity and precision.

She fidgeted as he approached her. She screamed into the tape he had replaced as he ran the knife through her am. Tears filled her eyes but the bitch didn't cry. Soon, she would cry, and he would take pleasure in seeing her break.

"I am going to leave it there for you to learn some hard lessons," he smiled. He would return tomorrow, and by then, she would give him the answers he desired.

CHAPTER 9

CATHERINE'S HEAD ACHED. She hadn't had a decent sleep in days. She took a sip of the crappy airport coffee. The moment they boarded the flight she was going to fall asleep, and hope that she got some rest before they arrived in Singapore.

"I got you this," Max said, handing her a pink chewy toy. It was for Devi. She smiled at the thoughtful gift. She missed her puppy so bad. She'd had a video call with her, and it had made her laugh to see her puppy play around in anticipation of her returning home.

"When did the constable say he would get back to us?" Catherine asked. She had been cleared of any wrongdoing with regards to Dominic's death and

Megan's kidnap, as expected, and the constable had promised to keep them updated. It did piss her that he mainly spoke to Max, instead of her. If only he had sprung to action right after the ransack, she would be lounging on the beach with Megan by now.

"When we get to Singapore, I will call him for an update. That's fine, right?" he asked.

She nodded. They had gotten no leads by the time they left Cannes. She hated how much her peaceful trip had been ruined. She hated that she was in such a state. And even worse, she hated that Megan was in danger.

"You are doing the right thing going on this trip," Max reassured her.

However, she didn't think so. She would rather remain in Cannes and find her friend.

"That's our flight," she said as a female voice came over the speakers. She reached for her carry-on bag, and her mind reflected on earlier in the day when she had to put Megan's belongings together. She'd wanted to leave them behind at the resort, for Megan to have something personal to wear when she returned, but everyone had said it was best to send them down to Florida. Grudgingly she had sent them to her home.

Her phone buzzed and she went still for a moment before her entire body began to shake in fright.

"What is it?" Max asked, placing his arms around her.

Fear in her eyes, she handed him her phone. His eyes snapped as he read the text, which was a one-liner, *See you in Singapore.* His eyes frantically looked around, and she did the same, but the airport was rowdy. She didn't even know who she was looking out for. Everyone looked and seemed suspicious.

"I want you to be calm," Max whispered as he held her gently. She had no idea how she made it into the airplane. They were just in luck because the flight was off-season and there were few passengers giving them enough privacy. He sat her down at the window seat, then sat next to her.

"Take a deep breath," he said calmly.

She breathed in deeply, and then out, but her heart still raced in fear. A man passed them, and she jumped, as she realized she was still holding on to Max's hands.

"It's going to be okay Catherine," he said confidently.

She shook her head. He had been right all along. She had not been safe in Cannes. The murderer and Megan's kidnapper had to have been watching her all along. How did he know she was going to Singapore? They had told no one except the chief where they were going to. And it had been a few minutes stopover at the police station before going to the airport. How had he also known about her coming over for a shoot at the winery? Whoever was playing these games, he was cold and ruthless, and it terrified her.

"He said he was going to see me in Singapore. That means he's here with us!" she said, sitting up to look around. Her eyes rested on an older couple who were talking in what sounded like Cantonese. There was a younger couple who had a two-year old with them. And then two young women who looked like they were related from their similar high cheekbones and brown eyes.

"You are not going to see whoever it is," Max said, gently nudging her down. She gave him a look and he shrugged. "They are good at what they do."

"Maybe we should go back to Florida," Catherine said. But then she decided not. This criminal could follow her home as well. The thought of such evil knowing where she lived made her shudder. "What if they are a syndicate?" she thought aloud.

Max gave her a look.

"If he was watching me, then somebody has to be watching over Megan, right?" Catherine asked.

"Yeah," Max said dryly. It was clear he didn't trust her line of thought.

"You should call the constable. Let him know what happened, and my theory," Catherine said.

"I will call him when we get to Singapore," Max said, flashing a smile at the hostess as she walked past them.

"How can you be so calm about this!" she snapped. Or was it because he was not the one being followed by a deranged murderer and kidnapper?

"Because there's nothing to worry about. Whoever it is loves playing mind games. He's doing this to upset you, and it is clearly doing so. I want you to be calm. You are going to be fine. I am going to make damn sure of it. Now why don't you put on your seat belt, and try to get some sleep?"

She had no idea how he was this calm, while she was perturbed. If he wasn't here, she would be look-ing around for a police officer to put her into protective custody, or whatever they called it.

"Here, take this," Max said, putting one of his earphones in her ear. She sighed as the calm soothing music filled her. It was an RnB song, and somehow Max had an amazing music taste. She closed her eyes as the plane took off, and allowed herself to let go in the sky, putting aside her fears and problems.

They landed in Singapore in the early hours of the following morning, giving them enough time to rest for the gala in the evening. She felt well rested, but the moment they picked up their bags from arrival, she was agitated, throwing looks around as they headed out of the airport.

A man, wearing an excited broad smile stood at the entrance of the airport with a huge banner that read, "Welcome to Singapore Catherine!"

Catherine sighed. How was she supposed to remain lowkey when she could not even leave the airport quietly?

"Welcome! Welcome!" he said as he hurried over to her. He was followed by a younger man who she suspected was his son from the resemblance. However, he looked bored, lacking the excitement of the older man.

They took their bags, leading them out to the curb where a limousine was parked. Max whistled, obviously pleased with the welcome treatment. Catherine rolled her eyes, trying to hide the fact that she was impressed.

This was her first time in Singapore. It was a beautiful city with high rise buildings and a lot of people. She had her eyes glued to the window as she took in all the beauty of the oriental city.

The hotel was a huge building, over twenty stories, and was certainly had to miss with its golden hue. Golden dragons sprouted water as they pulled into the parking area. The reception was a delight and she stared up in awe at the golden chandeliers that glistened when light struck the jewels. The lobby was enormous, probably the largest she had ever seen. People moved up and down, and she heard a lot of language as she looked around taking it all in. English, Chinese, Japanese… she lost touch.

At the front desk was a young man with a tag that read Xao. "Welcome to the Bridge," he said in Chinese.

Catherine lifted a brow when Max spoke back to him in fluent Chinese, and did not stumble.

He shrugged. "I picked it up some time ago," he simply said.

A young woman took over from the driver. She was pretty with translucent pale skin, and a slender body, Catherine wondered if she even ate in a day. They took the elevator up to the tenth floor, and walked down a long hallway which was lined with artworks from all around the world.

"Kindly call 211 if you need anything. We hope you enjoy your stay," the woman smiled as she stopped in front of their room door, handing Max a keycard.

"Where's your room?" she asked as she walked into the room. It was a suite she realized as she walked into a large living room with dark hues. "You are staying here with me?" she asked quietly, spotting two doors opposite each other.

"Yes. I changed the rooms arrangement for safety reasons. We need to stick together. I mean if that's okay with you. Do you have a problem with that?" Max asked.

"Umm… No, but I don't want my presence to hinder you from having a good time here," Catherine said.

He just stared back at her blankly.

"I mean if you want to bring a lady over," Catherine continued, silently telling herself to stop talking. She gulped as he took a step closer to her, and then another. Until there was barely any space between them.

"I assure you, I am bringing no woman over," he said in a whisper.

Her eyes closed and she realized her hands were shaking when he pulled away from her. What on earth was that? Why was she feeling warm all over? Why in that moment had she wanted to reach for him? God! This was damn frustrating!

She reached for her phone to send a message to Megan and sighed with the realization that she couldn't. Times like this she would pour it all out to Megan who would give her advice.

Max signaled to her to remain at the entrance. She watched him as he made his way around the room, checking behind the curtains; the space under the table which wouldn't even fit a toddler. Then he went to her bedroom and from the doorway she watched him look around. And then he checked his room as well.

"All clear," he said giving her a thumbs up.

She could not recall if he had mentioned being in the military, because the way he had gone about ensuring they were safe was so mechanical, his eyes alert, and his fists curled. It was strange seeing him in this light, but then he had always looked after her right?

She groaned in frustration as she laid on the bed in her room. Was she doing the right thing by being here? Especially now that whoever had taken Megan was also in Singapore too. Max had told her not to worry, that the person who had sent her the message was calling bluff, but what if he wasn't? What if all of this really had to do with her? She'd had crazy fans back in the days, but none of them were crazy enough to do such a thing. Perhaps they were looking at all of this from the wrong angle; she was probably the one who was supposed to have been taken. But then none of it added up or made sense.

She jumped at a knock on the door and realized that she hadn't even removed her clothes from her bag.

"I will be with you in twenty minutes!" she called to Max.

Room service delivered breakfast a couple of minutes later. She was hungry she decided as she wolfed down two sandwiches.

"What? I was hungry! I still am! Don't judge me," she teased as she threw Max a look when he flashed her a grin.

He chuckled. "It's good seeing you eat well, you have been picking at your food for the past days," he pointed out.

"Have you checked in on the constable?" she asked.

"There has been no new development. I am sure he will give us an update, when necessary," Max said.

Catherine sighed as she took a mouthful of sandwich. She hated the silence from Megan's end. She had always known that her friend would never leave without a message, but even if by some luck of fate she had, she would have passed across a message to her.

"Why not give him another call?" Catherine suggested.

Max sighed. "Catherine, he's going to call if there is any new update." His phone buzzed and she sat up in excitement. "It is the stylist, they are going to be here in five hours to prep you for the gala. You need to get more rest before then."

"I am well rested," Catherine disputed.

He gave her a look which made her smile.

"Well, I could go exploring," she said, covering a yawn.

"I would advise you don't go alone. At least not until we know who sent that message," Max said.

Catherine frowned. "I thought you said not to worry about the message?" she asked.

"It is not for you to worry about," Max said. She watched him go to the door to double-check that it was locked. "See you by two," he said, walking into his bedroom, and shutting the door close.

She rolled her eyes. He had always seemed straight-forward, but Max of the past days confused her. It was like… he was keeping something from her, and that upset her. What if he was going to drop her as a client? She couldn't deal with two losses in a matter of days. She scolded herself. She hadn't lost Megan. Her friend was going to return soon, she assured herself.

Catherine tried to get some eye-shut, but she could not sleep. There was too much going on in her mind. The text had her more upset than she liked to admit. While Max called it bluff, she knew it wasn't. Someone had followed her all the way to Singapore; this she was sure of. She had to be careful here in the city, because she did not know much of her way around. Neither was she good with the language. Times like this she wished she had taken up gun shooting like Max had suggested she do in the past. She had never been a guns type of girl, but it didn't seem like a bad idea at that point in time.

The room was quiet, and she tossed about, until she decided there was no need lying in bed, wasting her time. She headed out to the living room; Max stood by the window, on the phone, talking to someone quietly, she could not make out his words.

"I will call you back later," he said, ending the call.

"You don't have to stop talking to your girlfriend on my account," she teased with a smile.

"I don't have a girlfriend," Max said, as he poured some whiskey into a glass. He handed it over to her and she lifted a brow. "I guess you couldn't sleep. A lot on your mind?"

She nodded as she took a sip from it, wincing at the strong taste, as it hit her throat. "What about you?"

"Couldn't sleep as well," he said as he settled into a couch.

"Do you…" her words trailed as she shook her head.

"What is it Cathie?" he asked.

"Do you think she's still alive?" she asked with a gulp.

His silence scared her even more. The possibility of that being the outcome of all of this was one she had been refusing to think of. That her best friend was dead? No, she would rather cling on to the hope that Megan was alive, fighting hard to escape from wherever she was being held.

"I don't know Cathie," Max said, pouring some whiskey into a glass for himself.

She swallowed. He couldn't look her straight in the eye. She knew already what he thought. It was the reason he wasn't concerned about finding her.

"I want to find her Cathie, more than you even know," Max said, as if reading her thoughts. "But I don't know if she's alive or dead Cathie. The police are working hard to find her alive."

Catherine scoffed. Yeah right. The constable had not seemed serious about the matter until one of his people died. She didn't think he could find Megan, but then what else could she do?

"This is stupid to ask, but do you know anyone in the feds?" Catherine asked.

Max coughed, spluttering out some of his drink. "What did you say?" he asked with a strained voice.

"Like the FBI, or CIA," Catherine shrugged.

"The KGB as well huh?" Max lifted a brow.

"Haha, I am just saying that they could send their agents to look for her right. She's an American citizen, and I don't think that constable is qualified enough to find Megan," Catherine said.

"I am pretty sure the FBI and CIA have a lot to do Catherine. And the constable is qualified. He used to be a big-time detective in London before he retired home. He solved a lot of crimes back then," Max said.

She didn't bother to ask how he knew that, although she doubted the constable had bragged about his past experiences. The man hadn't impressed her a bit.

Max's phone rang and he stared at the caller, and then at Catherine. "Who's calling?" she asked, already knowing who it was.

He responded by answering the phone. "Hello constable. Yeah, thanks for calling."

"Put it on speaker," Catherine whispered.

"I am putting this on speaker so Catherine can hear what you have to say," Max said, making Catherine roll her eyes. Had that really been necessary?

"Have you found Megan?" Catherine asked excitedly.

"No, we haven't," the constable said.

Catherine sighed. So why was he calling now? "What of the man who took her? Have you found him?" she asked in a rush.

"We have not found him as well. We have put up a sketch of the man the waitress at the coffee shop saw her with, but no one has come up with more information. The sketch is not enough for us to get through our database," the constable explained.

Catherine groaned. Then why on earth was he calling?

"So what do you have for us?" Max asked.

"We spoke to Dominic's friends. He told them he was going to leave town, go to Paris for college. He didn't tell them where he was going to get the money from, but he was really excited and sure he was going to be rich. We think your guy made him some huge money to deliver the note," the constable said.

"I recall his wallet was empty when he was found. Any call records from his network provider?" Max asked.

"Yes, from a burner phone. The first call came in the morning she flew into Cannes. Then two calls came in the day of the kidnap, one in the morning, a couple of minutes before the note was delivered, and then a few hours later in the afternoon. And that was it," the constable said.

"He must have called to meet him for a balance of what was promised to him, and killed him. Any idea where he went to after he left the resort?" Max asked.

"We suppose it was straight to the woods. It is easy to walk to by the locals here, and it can be quite empty in the early mornings. There are no cameras around, but I assure you that we have gotten cameras stationed there now."

"So, you know nothing about where Megan is?" Catherine snapped.

Max shot her a look and she shrugged. The constable might as well not have called then, because he had provided no valuable information. The only thing she wanted to hear from him was that they had found Megan and had been taken to safety.

"We are working hard to find her. My men and I haven't had a decent rest in days," the constable said.

Surprisingly, his assurance gave Catherine some sort of calm. "Thank you," she mumbled.

"Just keep us updated," Max said.

"I should go get some rest, I have a long night ahead," Catherine said. She headed back to her room, and this time around, she was able to get some eye-shut.

The living room was a bey hive of activities. A wardrobe of clothes had been brought in, and a huge makeup box was opened with Ellen, a celebrity artist working on her face. Flashes of camera were in her face as the cameraman took pictures of the BTS.

She was having a good time as she prepped. She had a glass of wine in one hand and had taken some delicious rolls dipped in honey. It tasted great. This background to the glitz and glamour was something she liked.

"Amazing!" Ellen smiled, taking a step back.

Catherine liked her look. She had done a smoky look for her eyes, with a bright red lipstick that blended with her complexion.

"It's time to get you dressed," Saul, her stylist said. He held up a gorgeous blue dress with sequins. She had tried it earlier and it was a perfect fit.

With the help of her stylist and his assistant, she slipped into the dress. The long dress stuck to her curves like glue; the back was open, lined with white pearls.

"Amazing!" Saul clapped in delight.

She laughed at his excitement. The laugh stopped as she stared across the room. She swallowed, her heart raced in excitement. Staring at her was Max, and God! The way he looked at her, a luring look that she could not look away from; one that held her enthralled, sending shivers all over her body.

"We hope you tag us on Instagram," Saul said as he and the others began to clear out from the room.

In a matter of minutes, the room was empty. Except for her and Max. She took all of him in, and God did he look hot! The black tuxedo covered his well-built body, spreading across his broad shoulders. He had cleaned up, well most of the beards on his face had been shaved. His curly black hair was sleeked back, and she could not help but wonder whether his eyes had always been that intense.

"Hey," he said quietly, as he took steps closer to her.

"Hey," she whispered back, her heart racing faster with every step he took towards her. Her throat went dry and her tongue flickered out as he stood in front of her.

"You look really amazing," Max said, flicking a stray strand of her hair back.

"You don't look bad yourself," Catherine complimented.

He went quiet, staring at her, and she basked in his strong masculine scent. If he took her in his arms right now and kissed her, she would let him. She would wrap her arms around him and…

"Turn around," he said quietly.

She gulped, looking at him confused. He held up a diamond necklace. "You should wear it," he said.

It was a gift from Blues, a jewelry company she was signed to as an ambassador. She nodded, and with her whole body shaking in excitement turned around.

Her body went still as she felt the cold jewelry on her neck. And then… his warm hands. She could feel his breath on her. She fought back the urge to moan, as her body burned up with desire from within.

"Cathie?" he called to her, pulling her away from her thoughts.

She looked at him with wide eyes, hoping he did not see how much she wanted him in that moment.

"We should go," he said, offering his hand to hers. She slipped her hand into his, and she stopped shaking, comforted by his presence. "Stay with me, I don't want you out of my sight any time in the night," Max instructed as they headed out of the door.

Twenty minutes later, they arrived at the Benefit Gala. As the limo pulled in through the gate, they were greeted by camera flashes, with fans shouting out to them. It made her smile as she waved to them. The Benefit Gala was an international fashion event held yearly in Singapore. It was a charity event, and the proceeds were donated to a charity selected by the board members. This year, Catherine had been invited as a guest. Well, she had been pushing to be invited to one, but it was not until a couple of days when Max came to Canne that he told her the good news, she had gotten an exclusive invite to the show. How much she had always wanted it, and as she stepped out of the car to the red carpet, she told herself to enjoy the moment. All other worries would wait.

They were greeted by Stefan, one of the board directors, who kissed her on both cheeks.

"It is so great to see you Catherine! I have followed your works for many years," he said.

The crowd drew apart as she walked on the carpet. There were more flashes of light from the media as she posed, putting her leg out in the front as was her signature style. She waved, blowing kisses at the group of fans who had come out here to celebrate. As she was ushered off the red carpet, she looked out for Max, but she could not see him amidst the crowd going back and forth.

"Do you know—"

She jumped as a man pushed into her, almost tripping her if not for the usher who steadied her. She could barely get a glimpse of him as he went into the crowd. It was only when she was able to steady herself properly that she realized that a piece of paper had been shoved into her hand.

Her heart raced in excitement as she unrolled the paper. Written on it was an address: *7, Xing street, Chinatown, 12 noon tomorrow.*

Her eyes narrowed at it. What did this mean? She caught what seemed to be a glimpse of the man and went after him, finding herself in a long hallway that was deserted.

"Hey you!" she called after a man who ducked into a room. As she went down the hall, the lights overhead began to flicker, and her palms began to get sweaty.

"Hello!" she called out, her voice echoing down the hall. There was no response. She jumped as an arm circled around her wrist. She jumped, her heart almost popping out as she turned around.

"Oh God!" her hand flew to her chest. It was Max, and he wasn't pleased to see her there.

"What are you doing here? I told you not to get out of my sight!" Max snapped. "You are taking pictures one minutes, and then I can't see you!"

"Don't yell at me, I am not a child," she glared at him.

"Then stop acting like one, and care for your safety," Max scolded.

How dare he! She fumed as she stormed off, back to the party. Deep down, she knew he was right. She had been terrified in that hallway. What if that had not been him who had come at that moment? What if it had been Dominic's killer? All it would have taken was one moment and he would hurt her. But still, that didn't warrant him yelling at her like she was a five-year old.

Guests were socializing when she returned to the party. She shoved the note into her bag, she would deal with it later. Her face lit up with a smile as she spotted a couple of models from her youthful days.

"Rabbi!" she said, hugging a tall and gorgeous model from Sudan. In all her years of modelling career, she had the most pronounced cheekbones ever. In her fifties, the woman still looked divine. She really did need to share her skin and lifestyle regimen.

"I was so excited when I saw you were going to be here Catherine. You look so gorgeous!" Rabbi complimented.

"If it isn't my favorite girls in the world," a tiny voice said behind them.

They turned around, squealing in delight as they spotted Penny, a British model. Years ago, they had walked the stage for several international brands for almost five years in a row. How times had gone past; then they had been young, and had taken the world by a storm. Those were the days they didn't have to worry much; the gigs had come abundantly, and they had been the one on the upper end, choosing who and what they wanted to work on.

"It's been so long since we last saw each other," Rabbi said, as she took a selfie of the three of them.

They were seated at the same table which was an awesome way for them to catch up. They exchanged stories of where they had been in the past years. Rabbi was now a grandmother, and she showed them pictures of her pretty grandkids.

"Well, I am onto my third divorce. In a new relationship, she's great, and we are thinking of getting married, but I am not sure yet," Penny said, taking a glass of champagne which, she drained at a ridiculous fast pace.

"What about you Catherine? You must have the men feeding off your fingertips," Rabbi teased.

Catherine chuckled. "Well, I don't know about that. I have been quite busy with work," Catherine said.

"Yeah, you really have a lot going on for yourself, and I have to give it to you. It isn't easy for us models as we get older," Penny said with a sad look in her eyes.

In that moment, Catherine was grateful. Despite her complaints, she knew she had it easier than a lot of older models in the industry. She still got gigs, and she had her businesses. Some models were completely ignored by the fashion industry, despite paying their dues in their younger years. Some of them had squandered their wealth in their youth, without saving for the later years, and in their old age, they were having a tough time adjusting.

"Damn! That man is fine!" Penny whistled, her eyes past their table.

Even Rabbi who was happily married nodded in agreement. Catherine followed their gaze. It was no surprise when they rested on Max. He was seated a few tables away, with a direct view of her. Butterflies danced in her stomach as he held her gaze. He lifted his glass of champagne in a toast and she looked away flustered.

"Ohh… he's yours," Penny said with a hint of jealousy.

"That's Max, he's my manager," Catherine explained.

"Uhh… I see. I wish I had that type of manager," Penny said, earning a giggle from Rabbi.

"Come on Penny, it's not like that. Max and I are just friends," Catherine found herself explaining, but it seemed the ladies didn't believe her.

"Do you know my first marriage was to my manager?" Penny asked with a grin.

Catherine sighed, totally giving up. But she could not help but spare a look at Max, who again was watching her. Yeah, things with her and Max were definitely platonic, and they would continue to remain that way, she told herself.

It was a couple of minutes after midnight when Catherine returned home. She was alive, after all the dancing and glasses of wine. It had been great out there tonight after a couple of crazy days. She had no idea how much she had missed hanging out with the old girls, until tonight. They needed to do more of that, she assured herself. Despite the years that had passed, they were still her friends.

"Did you have fun?" she asked Max as they stepped into the living room. He had watched her all night long. Every time she looked at him, he was watching her. She hadn't even seen him dance or socialize with anyone.

He nodded, and she rolled her eyes. Now that she even thought of it, Max barely had fun at events he came along with her to. Most times, he didn't even drink. It was crazy how he was in the glitz industry, and he relegated himself to the background. He got the contracts for her, got her paid, but he didn't want to share even a glimpse of the limelight with her.

"Are you sure about that?" she teased as she moved closer to him. A big mistake because his scent masked her, making her sigh in contentment.

"You should have some rest. We have a long day ahead of us tomorrow," Max said, as he moved towards his room.

She reached for him, circling her arm around his wrist, stopping him. He turned to her with those intense eyes of his and she stared back at him.

"Your eyes are pretty," Catherine said, as if realizing that for the first time.

Max chuckled. Wait, was that a blush? "Thanks. Are you sure you haven't had too much to drink?"

"You know I didn't. You have been watching me all night long, right?" she asked as she moved closer to him.

"Catherine…" he warned in a hiss as she pressed her body against him. "Catherine, we can't—"

She made the first move, putting her arms around him, as she….

The buzzing of a phone separated them. It took a moment for her to realize that it was her phone ringing. She quickly reached for it, with one thought it was Megan calling. She sighed when she saw who was calling. It was her mother.

"Hi Sally," she said with a frown.

"Hello Catherine, it's been such a long time you know. You don't call anymore," Sally said.

Catherine sighed. It was Sally, her mother. Hadn't she called her like a month or so ago? Catherine could not recall. Catherine had left home when she was eighteen. She had left the small town of Armada, with a backpack and headed to New York to pursue a career in modelling. She had determined to have a better life, and get away from her family, especially her mother.

Catherine's parents had divorced when she was five years old. Her mother had moved in with her grandparents who owned a ranch. Best to say, Catherine had been raised by her grand folks, as her mother didn't really give a shit, with a preference for looking for more eligible bachelors. Two years later, she had remarried a judge's son, offering her the better life she had craved for, a Southern housewife. As she began a new family, she had forgotten Catherine. Or had she really? She had looked down on her daughter as not fitting into her new life. Even after her grandfather had died, followed shortly by her grandmother when she was fifteen, Sally had told Catherine she would give her up for adoption if the opportunity came. For the next two years, Catherine had lived with Sally and her family; it had been torture, with the woman treating her like trash. In the past years, she could count how many times she had called the woman who was her biological mother.

"What do you want?" Catherine asked. She knew the woman wanted something. It was the only time she called.

"Your sister is getting married," Sally said.

Yeah, Sally had two children after Catherine, Manny and Gina. Kids she absolutely adored, unlike her first child. Catherine had had somewhat of a relationship with them when she had been younger, but in the past years, their relationship had drifted apart.

"Congratulations to her. Is there anything else?" Catherine asked, staring at Max who had poured for himself a generous glass of whiskey.

"You have to be there, you could bring in some of your friends. Like Feely, the musician, he's a friend of yours, right? We have been trying to get him to perform at the wedding, but he's totally booked and expensive," Sally chuckled. "But if you talk to him, I am sure he can do it to us as a favor right?"

"Seriously?" Catherine sighed. Of course! She hadn't expected any better. "You haven't spoken to me in weeks, and you call me because of this? You really are unbelievable Sally."

"Come on. Do it for your sister, you haven't been much of a big sister to her you know," Sally said.

"I am going to ignore we had this call. I am going to end it now before I say something I can't take back," Catherine said.

"Is everything okay?" Max asked.

She nodded. "Just my mom being her normal self. So…" her voice trailed on as she stared at him.

"Yeah, that was a mistake," Max said, and she lifted a brow as he went on. "Lots of drinks tonight, emotions in play. We should call it a night. We have a long day ahead of us."

He was really going to blame the chemistry between them on a couple of glasses? She wasn't drunk; she had known what she was doing when she kissed him. "Good night Max," Catherine said with resignation. She didn't have the will to debate their attraction with him, especially after the call with her mother.

She took a quick bath and slid under the covers. Tonight, felt different, the bed felt much bigger and colder than it was the night before. She rolled over to the other side and wished for a faint moment that she had someone to share the bed with.

She went silent at approaching footsteps. They stopped in front of her doors and she could see the shadows from underneath the door. She sat up quietly, did he want to come in? To join her? Because she had no opposition to that. However, his footsteps retreated and she heard his room door open.

It was only as her eyes drifted to sleep, that she remembered the note in her purse. But she was lured by sleep, and reminded herself that she would deal with the note the following morning.

CHAPTER 10

CATHERINE WAS UP at five the following morning. Luckily, she didn't have much of a hangover. Well, Max had handed her a stainless flash, filled with a green murky drink which made her wince when she opened it.

"The perfect hungover cure," Max had grinned.

It tasted horrible, but five minutes later as they rode over to Marina Bay Sands, she felt pumped up for the day.

They were shooting early in the day before the sun came up. By the time they arrived, production had already set up their cameras and lightings. She was introduced to the director and the other crew, as well as the other casts who would be featured in the advert.

There was a diverse range of swim wears from costume, but they settled on a pink fringe one-piece. Her hair was curled and a bit of waterproof make up was done on her face. And then she headed out to do her job.

"Hey, there is a bit of an errand I need to run," Max said, pulling her to a corner.

"Umm… okay," she said.

"I should be back in an hour or more. Let me know how the shoot is going, and if I am not here by the time it is done, go back with Dan to the hotel. You see that guy?" he nodded at a tall skinny guy who was staring back at them. This was the first time she had seen him.

"Who's he?"

"He's a bodyguard, he's going to look after you when I am gone. He will follow you home if I am not back on time," Max said.

A bodyguard for what? He didn't even give her the time to challenge him, and he was off, while she glared at his back, and then at the bodyguard who retained a straight face.

Thankfully, it didn't take much time to shoot. Everyone brought their A-game, and well they were also experienced.

"Are you ready to return to the hotel?" the body-guard asked as she took a glass of champagne from a passing waiter.

"Not yet," she said. It had been a satisfying morning and she wanted to enjoy the pool and the sun. She laid on a lounge chair and pulled out her phone to take a couple of pictures. A hat on her head, she basked in the warmth and serene atmosphere.

"Shit!" she sat up as she remembered the note from last night. How could she have forgotten! She quickly reached for her bag and pulled out the note. She stared at it, and then stared at the bodyguard who was flirting with one of the models. She doubted he was going to let her go to the address. He would probably call Max the moment she even raised the issue up. And knowing Max, he would first be pissed at her, and would insist that she stayed put. But the note said to meet at 12 noon, and she had a couple of minutes left. She could not wait for Max, neither could she let this opportunity slip by. She had a strong feeling this was the way she would find her friend.

"I am going in for a change," she said to the body-guard who barely acknowledged her, his attention on one of the models, who was flirting with him. Who knew some woman would actually make him lose his gaze from her, she thought amused. She hurried to the rest room and slipped back into her clothes. Then she hurried out of the building, headed straight to the entrance.

A cab had just dropped off some teenagers, and she got into it. Whew! She let out a deep breath as the car pulled away. She had gotten away with that, she thought excitedly.

"Where to?" the driver asked.

She showed him the note. "Do you know it?" she asked. He nodded as he took a turn in the road. She occasionally looked at her phone for Max's call. She knew he would do so when he found out she had left without telling him her whereabouts.

They pulled up into a traffic congestion and she relaxed on the seat. She had no idea who she was going to meet when she got to her destination. What if she was walking into the enemy's den? She reached her bag and pulled out the butter knife she had taken off the caterer's table back at the pool. She was prepared, at least she hoped so, to defend herself if the need arose.

The cab took a turn into a tight busy street, where a dense traffic was building up. People dashed in front and behind the vehicle. A man holding what seemed to be bracelets stopped in front of her window, and gestured at her wildly. She didn't understand what he was saying, but it was clear he wanted her to buy from him. She shook her head, but that didn't stop him. Some other hawkers realized there was someone of interest and soon they crowded the other window, gesturing at her to buy their wares from them. Catherine looked ahead, but that still didn't stop them. She was more than grateful when the congestion eased, and the driver pulled away from the chaos.

"Welcome to Chinatown," the driver smiled apologetically.

A couple of turns down the busy neighborhood and he stopped in front of an old building. In front was a noodle shop, and the strong aroma drifted to her. The driver handed her his card after she paid him. "Call me when you want to leave," he said as she got out of the car.

She looked at the address in the note, and up at the name of the noodle shop. It was the same. Xing noodles. She just had five minutes left until the meeting time.

Catherine went still at a sensation. It felt like she was being watched. She could feel eyes on her, watching her. She looked around, but the crowd going and coming was too dense for her to make out who was watching her.

Curious eyes of the customers followed her as she walked into the noodle shop. Seated out front were customers drinking and eating noisily. It was not rare to see a white woman in these parts, but they were usually accompanied, and didn't look as glam as she did. She headed straight for what seemed to be the front desk, a beat counter where a woman argued with a customer. By the side of the room was an older woman snoring pretty loud, Catherine wondered how she could sleep through the chaos.

"Soup?" the woman asked, beaming brown teeth at her.

She shook her head. "Umm... I am to meet someone here?" she said. She showed her the note and the woman shook her head.

Discarding her as a lost tourist, the woman continued arguing with the customer. Catherine sighed as she looked around the room which was almost clouded from the open pot of noodle on a cooker. There was not even a vacant place to sit. How was she supposed to wait for someone she did not even know?

She returned to the outside, and swatted a couple of flies that buzzed around her. Perhaps coming here was a mistake in the first place.

"Pssssstttt..."

She turned at the sound and frowned. The older woman who had been sleeping inside was now gesturing at her to follow her to the alley. Catherine hesitated, unsure of what was going on, but her curiosity waned, and she hurried after her.

The alley was busy, with traders selling, overwhelmed by aroma from nearby shops. Catherine hurried after the woman who surprisingly had a fast pace as she headed towards a dumpster.

"Do you know who invited me to come here?" Catherine asked when she got to the woman.

"For you," the woman said, thrusting a brown envelope at her, and then she was gone into the alley.

Catherine stared at the sealed envelope. What was inside? She could feel something like papers? Or were they photographs? There was only one way to find out. She froze at that sensation of being watched. Putting the envelope under her arm, she hurried out of the alley, only to bump into…

"What the hell do you think you are doing?" Max snapped, grabbing her arm. She had never seen him this angry, his eyes wide, and his nostrils flared as he glared at her.

"What… What are you doing here?" she asked in surprise.

"I gave you an instruction! Go to the hotel immediately! Don't you Have the fucking dumbass bodyguard with you. But what the hell did you do!" he yelled.

Her face turned red as curious eyes of the customers and passers-by settled on them. She wondered how he had found her.

"I… I was going to tell you…" Her excuses were weak, and they both knew it. She had messed up by coming here, but best believe he would have insisted she did not come here.

"What is that?" he glared, eying the envelope.

"It is none of your business—"

It was too late as he grabbed it from her, opening it before she could stop him. His eyes calmed down immediately he pulled out the content. He stared at her in worry and before he could take it from her reach, she grabbed the first photograph.

"Oh my God!" Her knees went weak, and if he did not hold her that moment, she would have hit the floor. In the picture was Megan; her darling Megan pinned to the wall with large knifes pinning her bloodied arms to the wall. Her eyes were open and empty, and her face was drained of blood. Gone was the exciting and vibrant Megan she had always known. The Megan in that picture was dead.

"Let me see!" she cried as she grabbed the other pictures from Max. They were similar, of Megan in death; close up shots of her lifeless body, with her eyes staring right at Catherine; they would always haunt her in years to come.

"She's dead! She's dead! Megan is dead!" Catherine burst into tears as her worse nightmare had become true. Her best friend had been murdered.

"It's okay Catherine," Max pleaded as more eyes settled on them with greater curiosity.

"Nothing is okay! It is not fucking okay!" Catherine yelled at him.

He grabbed her arm, pulling her to a waiting car by the curb which she hadn't noticed. Driving it was the bodyguard who scowled at her, but she cared nothing for his displeasure as tears rolled down her eyes.

"Take us to the hotel," Max instructed as he slid next to her.

Catherine felt cold inside. She had held on to hope that Megan was still alive. She had believed that somehow this was some silly joke that would be unraveled when Megan returned. But now she was met with the truth that her friend was dead. How could this happen? How the fuck! She thought as she sobbed harder.

"Megan is dead," Catherine whispered in disbelief.

"We are going to find out who did this," Max said, but his assurance did nothing to calm her. All she wanted was to see Megan alive, to see her friend smile and tease her. That was the only thing that mattered.

She had no idea when they got to the hotel. She was still in shock as they headed into the elevator, with Max holding her firmly, probably afraid she was going to faint.

Catherine had met Megan at a coffee shop fifteen years ago in downtown Florida. She had just gotten off a hectic shoot which had been up all night long. She had been on the line trying to get coffee when there was an argument behind over who was standing there and who was not. Catherine had seen Megan join the line before the skinny dude who called Megan a bitch. Oh, Catherine had rained hell on him, her and Megan a force that had made the dude turn around and leave the coffee shop.

Megan joined her while she enjoyed her coffee and doughnut, and they laughed about how tough they had been. It turned out they lived close to each other, and the following weekend they had gone shopping. Friends came and went, and so did family, but in all that fifteen years, Megan was the only stable person that was in her life. And now she was gone.

"Shhh… it's going to be all right," Max comforted her as he sat her down on her bed.

"She's gone Max. My best friend is dead," Catherine sobbed. All this time she had been having fun, her friend was being hurt. Maybe if she had remained in Cannes to look for her, she would still be alive. If she hadn't invited her to Cannes, she would still be alive, working her hectic job. This was all because of her, she cried.

"It is not your fault Cathie, you need to know this. Whoever this did planned way ahead, and it was premediated," Max explained, but it did nothing to reduce the responsibility she felt for Megan's death.

"Hey, look at me," Max cleaned the tears rolling down her face as he lifted her face to his. "It is not your fault," he repeated.

"I need… I need…" She had no idea what really she needed in that moment. For Megan to come back? For some sort of comfort? She made the first move, kissing him. For a moment, she thought he would push her away, but he took her lips, and push them firm toward his.

His fingers danced around her neck, drifting lower and lower, until they hovered over her blouse.

He pulled away from her for a moment, shrugging out of his jacket. wow! He had an amazing body! Even much better than she had imagined, well-toned abs, and a broad chest, and was that a tattoo, she squinted, but was distracted as he reached for her again, placing her hands on his chest.

She felt… way better than she had felt in a very long time.

Catherine rolled over on the bed with a smile. Making love with Max had been amazing. Damn! That was an understatement. It was the best ever, or was she just being clouded by her grief? Her eyes opened as it hit her what had led to their love-making. Megan! She turned to the side of the bed, Max wasn't there. She reached for her robe and put it around her body then headed out of the room.

Max was on a call when she walked into the living room. "I just sent the pictures over to you. This is now a serious investigation and I need you to escalate," he said sternly to whoever it was on the other end of the phone. "I will call you back," he added, his eyes resting on Catherine.

"Hey," Catherine said shyly, pulling the lapels of the robe. She felt shy under his gaze, which was silly since about an hour ago they had been deeply kissing.

"How do you feel?" he asked, with a concerned look.

"I don't know," she admitted, pouring a healthy amount of whiskey into a glass. Her eyes fell on the pictures scattered on the table and she winced. She did not like seeing Megan that way. Sensing her upset feelings, Max gathered the pictures, shoving them into the envelope. But that did nothing to remove the images of Megan from her mind; they would always be there.

"Who were you talking to?" she asked.

"The constable in Cannes," he said.

She scoffed. If he had done his job right from the moment she called him to the hotel, she was pretty sure Megan would be alive. Damn him!

"It is not the constable's fault either," Max said.

Catherine glared at him. Yeah right. "He can't do anything. He's slow, incapable, and everything you can even mention."

"I have also spoken to someone who's going to get through to the American embassy. They are going to take control of the case. We are going to find who killed Megan," Max said reassuringly. "Now Cathie, you have been hiding a lot from me. You did not go to Chinatown and stumble upon those pictures by chance," he said with a fixed look.

"Yesterday at the gala, someone gave me a piece of paper. Look, he bumped into me and gave it to me," she quickly added, sensing that he was not pleased. "I would have told you, but you are so uptight these days, I don't even know what's going on with you," she explained.

"And so you decided to go there on your own? What if he had hurt you huh? Or taken you just like Megan? Did you think of the possibilities?" Max asked.

"I had a knife with me," Catherine said weakly, getting an eyeroll from him.

He moved to her, pulling her into his arms. "I need you to be safe Cathie, and that means no going out by yourself. This is not a Martin van Helden storybook, we are dealing with a real-life sociopath here. I can't be with you all the time, so I need you to promise that you will be careful, and that if you find anything, you will let me know," he said.

She looked up at his concerned eyes. "Okay, fine," she muttered getting a nod from Max. she knew he was going to hold her to her words. "So, what happens now?" she asked. They didn't even know where Megan was. She would like to bring her back to Florida, for her to be properly buried. The thought of saying goodbye finally to her friend made her eyes well in tears.

"The pictures are going to be scrutinized to know where she is, and they are going to cover more grounds in Cannes. An autopsy will be done, before her body will be released. She had no one else right?" Max asked.

Catherine nodded. Megan was an orphan, and did not have any siblings. She had told Catherine a long time ago that she was listed as her next-of-kin and was the only beneficiary in her will.

"Just as you want to know everything that I stumble on Max, I need to know everything with regards to Megan. She was my friend, and I deserve closure," Catherine said.

"Of course, Catherine," Max said.

She pulled away from him and was suddenly conscious of herself and what had happened between them. She cleared her throat as she nervously flicked her hair back. "Umm… about what happened…"

"Let's not talk about that now Catherine. There's too much going on. When we get back to Florida, we can deal with all that has happened," he flashed a smile at her.

She agreed with him. She didn't understand what had happened today. Had she just been overwhelmed with her emotions, and he had no option than to comfort her? She didn't want to start thinking things over because she was not in the right head space. What mattered now was Megan; every other thing could wait.

Max's phone buzzed with a message, which he read silently. "Our plane leaves eight in the morning," he said.

She sighed with relief. As much as she had enjoyed her eventful time in Singapore, she could not wait to go back to the safety of her home. Here, she kept on looking over her shoulder. She did not feel safe, but back in Florida, she was pretty sure she would feel much safer.

"I have to get my things packed. I will see you in the morning," she said, turning around to her room.

THE WARM AIR hit Catherine as she emerged from the airport with her bags. She breathed in the city of Florida and sighed with content. Far and wide, home was the best. She turned to Max who had opened the door of their cab for her to get in.

"Thanks Max," she said to him with a grateful smile. She was grateful to him for making her feel wanted again with the gigs she had been involved in. Being a part of the limelight had made her relive her younger days, and made her remember why she had gotten into modelling in the first place.

He returned her smile. "Just doing my job," he said.

She wanted to ask him if screwing her was part of his job description but she decided not. Best to hear the answer. "When are we going to the cops?" she asked.

"You need to get rested first. You have been busy this past week," Max pointed out.

"There's no time to waste," Catherine said. It was best to make hay while the sun shone.

"Let's do tomorrow. By then my contact at the embassy should have been able to get something concrete across," he said.

The cab pulled away from the airport and headed to the expressway. She was back home, without Megan, she thought with sadness. As much as she tried to put the pieces together, none of it made sense. Why had Megan's killer followed her all the way to Singapore? Surely, he could not have snuck Megan into Singapore and killed her? So why bother her? Was this some sick minded serial killer who liked to taunt the loved ones of his victims? Max had told her to think less of the theories, but she could not help herself. She felt like there was too much missing out for her to understand what was really going on. She wanted answers, and she bloody well hoped she got them.

"You don't have to follow me home," Catherine pointed out as they took the highway that led out of town.

"I insist," Max said.

She rolled her eyes at his chivalry. It wasn't as if he had been dropped home earlier the driver would stop in the middle of the road to hurt her. Well, she couldn't be always sure she thought as she stared at the quiet driver in the rearview.

Her heart leapt with joy as the structure of her home loomed ahead. The gates opened and the car drove into the compound.

"We see tomorrow," Max said as he helped her get her bags out of the car.

The front door opened and Devi came running out, flinging herself at Catherine who chuckled in delight. How much she had missed her girl, she thought as she littered her with kisses.

"Hope you have been such a good girl huh?" she asked, earning a bark from the dog. Spotting Max, the puppy left Catherine and headed to Max who rubbed her stomach. The dog rolled over in excitement, and Catherine shook her head amused. She didn't blame her, she would do the same if Max tickled her as well.

"I have to get going Cathie," Max said. He gave her a long look and it seemed like he wanted to say something, but he got into the car.

"Welcome home Cathie," Tehila said, helping her with her bags in.

Cathie looked around her home. It had just been about a week or more since she left, and it seemed like she had been gone for months. She had definitely missed home; her bed, the peace and calm of her home…

"I'm sorry about Megan," Tehila said.

Cathie nodded. It still felt like a dream, some exaggerated prank that was going to end any moment soon, when Megan jumped in front of her and yelled, "Surprise!" But deep down, she knew it was true. Her best friend was dead, and she was devastated with the realization.

"Have they found out who killed her?" Tehila asked.

Cathie shook her head. Investigations were undergoing in Cannes, with the American embassy involved. She was going to meet with some detective tomorrow to give her statement.

"Her bags are downstairs, they were delivered this morning," Tehila informed.

"Thanks," Cathie flashed a weak smile at her.

"Would you like anything? Lunch? Snacks?" Tehila asked.

Cathie shook her head. "I just want to rest, and be left alone for a while. I will let you know if I need anything."

The older woman gave her a thoughtful look, but respecting her decision left, closing the door softly behind her.

Cathie turned to Devi who cuddled to her. She looked up at her with those big brown eyes, and Cathie knew that Devi understood that she was going through a tough time.

"Yes Devi, Megan is dead, and I don't know what to do," Cathie said, as a tear rolled down her eye. She tried to wipe it, but more droplets came flowing down, and she was soon bawling her eyes out. Devi whimpered, placing her paw on her comfortingly, as if saying everything was going to be okay.

Cathie woke up early the following morning, almost an hour before her alarm went off. She stayed in bed, just staring into the distance. She did not feel like getting up, and going on with her routine. Was she supposed to act like everything was alright, when it wasn't? She knew that life had to go on, and this pissed her. Why couldn't the world stop revolving? Why couldn't the sun stop shinning? Megan was dead! She had been murdered! Surely there had to be an effect or a consequence, something had to happen right to show that a jewel had been taken from the world? It was damn cruel how the world just continued to move on, without any regard for a lost life.

She had breakfast quietly, her thoughts scattered all over. She had a lot to do with her return. Before going to Cannes, she had been working on a new scent, and had been rescheduling her meeting with the production company. Somehow, she needed to have that meeting done with. Also, she had been invited to be a judge at an upcoming modelling show. When was it? In two or three weeks? Was it too late for her to turn them down, and tell them to find someone else on the judging panel? She would have to ask Max if any contracts where going to be broken if she pulled out at this time.

A car pulled up in front of the house, and with the way Devi wagged her tail excitedly, she knew it was Max. Yeah, Max was another topic that troubled her mind. They hadn't spoken about that night. It seemed like it had not happened, but how could she forget she took a sip of her coffee and almost choked at how hot it was. She was already damn hot from the inside! The sex had been so freaking good, and just thinking about it bothered her.

"Hi Cathie," Max said as he headed in. Tehila lit up as she exchanged greeting with him. The woman was rather fond of Max, and always asked about him.

"Hi, hope you had enough rest," she said. He nodded, and she could not help but rake her eyes over him from head to toe. Damn! The man was fucking fine. He caught her gaze and lifted a brow, which made her smile to herself.

"Breakfast," Tehila said, placing a plate of scrambled eggs in front of Max.

That was fast, Catherine thought amused. But then Tehila liked to feed people. Every Wednesday, she worked at a soup kitchen, feeding homeless people.

"Any news?" Catherine asked.

"A special homicide unit has been assigned the investigation in Cannes. It is headed by a brilliant French detective. While our government sympathizes, they don't want to interfere with the investigation, but they are going to work with them." He checked his wrist watch. "We will be meeting with an official from the French government by ten. Just a bit of regularity."

"What about the FBI?"

Max went still at her question. "What happened with the FBI?" he asked quietly, staring at her oddly.

"Shouldn't this be escalated to them? Or is it the CIA, or Homeland?" she sighed. "I don't know. I just think our government should be actively involved in this. They need to find her!"

He covered her hand with his. "They are doing the best they can Cathie. There are laws in place, and we… the government can't overstep them. Trust the process huh?"

She sighed. How could she trust a process that had not saved her friend on time? A process that had her murderer out there, without being apprehended.

"Let's get this over with then," Catherine said.

Max drove a black Buick sedan. It was quite a plain and Catherine would say ugly vehicle. There was just nothing outstanding about it. Max chuckled as she slid into the passenger's seat with a frown.

"I hate your car," Catherine said for the hundredth time.

"She loves you, you know," he said, patting the dashboard, which made her roll her eyes.

She had asked him several times why he didn't buy something sleek and nice. He could afford it well enough, but he told her he liked the aesthetics, which always made her scoff.

"The judge panel, can I pull out of it?" she asked as they drove out of the compound.

"Having second thoughts?" Max asked.

She nodded. "I feel like I need my space. To be on camera for a couple of weeks is not something I think I am ready for," she admitted.

"But being alone in your own thoughts is not wise either," Max pointed out.

She sighed. He was right as well. She had been up for most of last night in her own thoughts, trying to figure out what the hell she was supposed to do to move on.

"I will call and let them know. They will be disappointed, but they will understand," Max said.

The rest of the ride was quiet, and Catherine appreciated that. She really wanted the murderer to be apprehended, and for him to face the electric chair immediately. She didn't want him to spend a day in prison; no, she wanted him to pay for his crimes.

"We are here," Max said.

They had pulled up in front of the French embassy with a French and American flag mounted above the front door. He took her hand before they stepped out the door. "Cathie, it is going to be okay. I am here with you," Max reassured her.

She nodded numbly at him.

They went through security and were led to a small office with a table and four chairs; two on the other side of each other. They waited for about five minutes when the door opened and a man and woman, in their forties came in. They introduced themselves as Nelson and Frances. Frances was a lawyer, and Nelson was former military, now working in law enforcement for the French government.

"We are sorry for your loss," Frances said.

"Have you found out who did this?" Catherine asked. That was all that actually mattered to her.

They shook their heads. "I assure you the French government is working hard to find the person who did this," Nelson said, but his confidence did nothing to reassure her. "We know you have given a statement, but we will like for you to take us through what happened when you were in Cannes."

Catherine rubbed her face in frustration. She hated reliving all that had happened, but it was all she did these past days. Think and wonder what she should have done different. She knew she couldn't go back in time, but perhaps, if there was a way to change things, there was so much she would have done. Like not going on that damned trip.

"I… I had a job to do at a local winery in Cannes, so I felt it was a great idea for Megan to come along as well. She works too hard, and her boss is an ass…"

Max coughed next to her, and did Frances actually chuckle? Yeah, she needed to rest more. "I was going to work for 2-3 days, then we were going to have a great time for the rest of the week. It was going to be fun…"

She pushed back tears, as she reached for the bottle of water on the table. She took a mouthful, as she willed her tears back. The last thing she wanted was to break down in front of this people. Be strong, she could hear Megan's voice in her head.

She went on to tell them all that had happened with the note, and leaving for the café, then coming back to the ransacked room.

"Did they take anything?" Frances asked.

She shook her head. "That's what made me suspicious. They took nothing from her room. Her money, jewelries, even her passport, they were all still there," Catherine said.

"Her bags, where are they now?" Nelson asked.

She frowned at him. That seemed like an odd question, but she ignored it. "I had them brought over to my home. I wanted to leave them behind at the resort, but decided otherwise. Will they be needed for the investigation? I don't think they are of any use," she said.

"Thanks for coming around, we will let you know if we need any information," Frances said.

"I want you to find the asshole who did this, and make him pay. Megan… not everyone understood her. She was amazing, the best person to have in your corner. She didn't deserve to die," Catherine said, unable to hold back her tears this time around.

"Are You okay?" Max asked, pulling up in front of her office about an hour later.

Catherine nodded. She was just tired, and it had nothing to do with physical fatigue. The meeting had drained her more than she expected. Everyone was talking, but there were no results.

"I should take you back home," Max suggested.

"No, I need to work," Catherine said. "Thanks Max," she flashed him a grateful smile. Although they were friends, this wasn't part of his job description, and in a matter of days he had been able to pull strings and get her escalate the matter.

"We need to talk Cathie," Max said, holding her gaze.

"Not now," Catherine said. Her emotions were too much in a twist to talk about what had happened between them. Besides, she was afraid of where the conversation would lead. Knowing Max, he would let her know that night had been a mistake, and they should forget about it. She didn't want to be rejected and most of all alone. It was best to keep the conversation at arm-length until she was ready.

"There you are! You look so good!" Henry cried as she walked through the front door.

He was such a liar, she thought, because she looked like crap.

"Welcome back," Natalie smiled.

"Your pictures game has improved. And so has your engagement on social media, I am still working on the analysis, but you are going to be the influencer of the year," Henry droned on.

"Are you okay?" Natalie asked, sensing her sadness.

"Megan is dead," Catherine said.

The room went quiet, and then…

"Oh my God! What happened?" Henry cried.

"You are joking right?" Natalie asked.

Henry considered Megan a wardrobe hazard, but they were both cordial with her, knowing that she held an important place in Catherine's life. The couple of times Megan had come around, Natalie had a great time making suggestions for Megan which she always went with.

Five minutes later, they all sat in her office, while Catherine gave them a summary of what had happened. The atmosphere in the room was tense, and Catherine didn't blame them.

"We are so sorry Catherine… I didn't even know," Henry said.

She had been tempted to make a post of losing her friend on social media, but she decided otherwise, knowing that there would be too much messages to deal with that she could not handle. Besides, of what use would the sympathizes be? They would not bring Megan back.

"This feels like some joke, but you wouldn't play like that," Natalie said. "Why don't you take some time off? We can handle the store," Natalie added, and Henry nodded in agreement.

"I don't want to be at home alone. I need to immerse myself in work, the good kind, so I don't think about her all the time," Catherine said, clapping her hands. "I think on that note, we should get started with work." She didn't like the pitying looks she was getting. She had never been one for pity any way.

"Let us know if you need anything," Natalie said.

For the rest of the day, Catherine immersed herself in work. Or at least she tried to, but several times she caught herself thinking of Megan. She imagined her dead in that room, far away from everyone else. What if they never found her body? What if she had been buried in the woods, where no one would find her?

It was late in the evening Catherine headed back home in a cab. Tehila was getting ready to leave for her weekly volunteering at the food bank. When she was done, she would go over to her daughter's place in the city to be with her family, then return the following afternoon. Her housekeeper was a recent widow, and it was not until after her husband died, and their home sold off to pay some debts she hadn't known he had been owing that Catherine suggested she moved into the house. It was a great arrangement and the woman looked forward to her day off when she spent time with her family.

"Are you sure you will be okay on your own?" Tehila asked. "I could call the shelter and let them know I won't be coming," she suggested.

"And leave hundreds of stomachs grumbling and pissed? Hell no, go Tehila, I will be fine," Catherine smiled, with a wave.

The house was quiet, well except for Devi who followed her closely. She had a light dinner by the pool side, then made dinner for Devi who slopped it all so quickly as if she was starving. She stayed out by the pool for a while, scrolling through her phones, going through pictures of her and Megan, well the few pictures she had anyway. She was tempted to delete them, so she could stop going through them, but she couldn't bring herself to do any of that.

It was dark when she finally went inside the house. She covered a yawn as Devi followed her upstairs. The moment her head hit the pillow, she was out.

Something woke Catherine. It was a sound downstairs. The creaking of the stairs or… she sat up in bed, her heart racing. Another bad dream, she was about to blame it on, but that sound came again from downstairs. It was certainly not Tehila, as she would not be back until tomorrow afternoon or evening. And it was not Devi who was now awake, her ears tensed as she listened. Catherine gestured at her to be quiet.

She quietly got out of bed and pulled on her robe. Her hands shook as she searched in the drawer for something. Her hand pulled out a taser. It had been gifted to her by Megan a couple of years back. "Top notch," Megan had said confidently. "It will knock a man out in a second."

On tiptoes, she carefully opened her room door, shutting the door behind on Devi, while signaling at her to remain in there. She didn't want her dog to get in harm's way, if it came to that.

It was dark, having put off all the lights before going to bed. But it was her home, and she knew her way in the dark. The noise was coming from her study; a small room which also doubled as her home office. It was the room Megan's bags were kept.

The door was open, and as she drew closer, there was no doubt where the noise was coming from. She stood at the doorway, her heart racing in panic as she peeped in. Ransacking the bags was a hooded figure.

Adrenaline rushed through her in that moment. But before she could lunge at him, she felt an arm wrap around her from behind. He was not alone! The arm around her neck tightened and she felt herself going unconscious. With every strength she had, she pressed the taser on her attacker. He let go of her, just as his accomplice ran past her.

He cried out in pain as he struggled to get up. She made a move towards him, retreating as he flashed a knife. For a moment, as she stared at his eyes through the hooded mask, she thought he was going to stab her.

"Bitch!" he muttered, right before running out.

Her heart pounded so fast, she thought it was going to explode. "Oh God!" she placed a hand on her chest. She felt… scared. And alive, with adrenaline rushing through her.

Quietly, she went down the hallway, into the kitchen. The back door was wide open. She reached for the kitchen phone and dialed the only person she could think of.

CHAPTER 12

CATHERINE'S HANDS SHOOK as she drank a glass of water. Her heart raced in excitement and fear, with Devi whimpering by her side, sensing her emotions. She looked down the hallway, to the door where it had happened. She had no idea when her feet moved, and soon she found herself hovering over the boxes.

She wasn't one for conspiracy theories, but this was not a coincidence. Barely a day after she returned, and Megan's things were brought over, and intruders broke into her home? Hell no! Something was going on, and it just didn't make sense.

She knelt down in front of one of the boxes, a duffel bag, recently bought by Megan. She zipped it open, fighting tears as she removed each one of Megan's clothing which she had packed back in Cannes. She had seen her friend wear most of these clothes. She was supposed to be alive, damn it!

There was nothing in the bag. And she went over the content twice. Her eyes settled on the other bag, a brown box, which Megan had had for a long time, probably over five years. It had a combination lock, a set of four numbers, which Megan had not used when they were in Cannes. She flipped the cover of the box open, running her eyes through the content. Again, like the other bag, there was nothing of interest, at least something that would warrant her home to be broken into. In frustration, she slapped the box close, kicking it.

She frowned as the box took its time moving an inch. That was weird, she thought, but shook it off, but then her mind dwelled on it again. She stood up and lifted the box, her frown deepening. She used to have a box similar to this, but it was not as heavy as this. Her eyes narrowed as she stared at the box.

"No way," she thought as an idea quickly settled on her mind. But then, what if there was a secret compartment in the box huh? Sitting next to the box, she ran her fingers over the top cover. There was nothing she could see or feel. She flipped it open and ran her fingers through a space by the cover dedicated for undies. There was nothing until… a small button, which she clicked on.

"Shit!" she muttered as the box clicked, separating the storage from the lid. Even though she was alone, she cast a glance around her, as she hurried to the other side of the box. Inside was a black humped envelope. She stared it for a moment, her breathing hitched. She should close it, and act like she hadn't seen anything, a part of her decided, knowing she was going down a rabbit hole, of which she had no idea where it would end. But her curiosity won over. She grabbed the black envelope just as the front bell rang.

Max wore a worried look as she opened the door. He quickly wrapped her in a hug. "Why did it take you so long to answer the door? I was about to kick it in!"

"I am fine," she said. She had gone upstairs and shoved the envelope in her safe, where no one could see it.

"I need you to lock yourself in and call the police while I scout the compound," he said, letting go of her.

She did as he said, returning to the living room where she nursed a cup of coffee. Ten minutes later, he was back. He held up a small black box. "They left this behind. Used it to hack through the security system."

Just then two police vehicles pulled up in front of the house. The next couple of hours were hectic for Catherine, as the cops trooped in, searching through the compound, and the library. As she sat in the living room, their voices moving back and forth, she could feel a raging headache building.

"Good morning ma'am."

She looked up at an older Latino man, probably in his sixties. He introduced himself as Diego. "I apologize for the inconvenience ma'am," he said, flipping a small notepad open. "We have identified their source of entry, the road by the side gate," he was referring to an untarred road accessible by a two-wheeler. "We found some tracks, probably belongs to a motorcycle. The padlocks were broken," he continued, answering her question as to how they had gotten past the gate.

"Tell me, do you have any enemies? I understand that you are a model and businesswoman, is there anyone you have gotten into a bad deal with recently? A disgruntled staff or handyman?"

She shook her head. "No, there's no one I can think of. And I don't believe they were here for me."

He looked at her questioning.

"My friend Megan was killed recently while we were on a vacation to Cannes. The intruders went after her belongings," Catherine pointed out.

Max cleared his throat as he joined them. "I don't think you should jump into conclusion Catherine, I mean—"

She sent him a look. "I know what I am saying. It all adds up. In all the years I have stayed here, this has never happened."

"Tell me more about your friend's death," the detective said with interest.

"We were in Cannes, at a resort. I was there for a shoot for a winery, and I invited Megan to be there so we could have some girl's time. I received a note one morning to meet up at a restaurant with the winery. When I returned, her room was ransacked, and she was gone. A couple of days later, I got pictures of her dead," Catherine summarized.

"And all of this happened in France?" the detective asked.

"I got the pictures while I was in Singapore. While at the airport I got a message from her killer that he was going to see me in Singapore."

"Then like you suspect, this is no isolated intrusion. It could all be connected," the detective said.

"We spoke to the consulate yesterday, but this happening..." her voice trailed on with the realization that she was not safe. Whoever had killed Megan had followed her from France, to Singapore and now to Florida. He was a crazy murderer, and that terrified her.

"The consulate has this covered, they are working with the local police," Max said.

The detective ignored him, directing his question to her. "Your friend's bags, we will would like to take them in with us, there could be something in them that would help us."

"I don't think that's a good idea," Max quickly said.

"Who are you again?" the detective glared.

"He's my friend and manager," Catherine defended. "And yes you can take the bags with you," she added, earning a disapproving look from Max. She was tempted to tell them what she had found, but decided otherwise. She needed to know what Megan was involved in, before she got others involved. Her friend was dead, and if she was involved in something shady, she didn't want to dent her reputation, or reveal something that could derail the cops from finding her killer.

"Thank you. In the meantime, I will have a security detail stationed outside your home. For a day or two, and I would advice you to probably get private security to cover all bases. There's one, I can recommend," he said taking out a card, which he handed over to Catherine. It read Bold Securities.

"When are you guys going to be done? Here, I mean, and well with your investigation?" Catherine asked.

"We are almost done. Five or ten minutes. And we can't tell with the investigation. It depends on a number of factors, but I will keep you informed. If there's anything you remember, or any information you would like to share, let me know," he said, handing her his personal card. He nodded at Max and walked away.

"I don't think giving them access to Megan's bags was a good call," Max said disapprovingly.

She held back telling him what she had found and said, "They need it for their investigation. Besides, I will get them back."

As promised, the police cleared the house seven minutes later. She was glad to see them, her home now quiet. She looked across the street, and could see the police cruiser parked out in front. It certainly did not make her feel safe, but when she turned around to Max, she did feel safe.

"I am going to spend the night here," he said, placing pillows on the couch. It was not a question, neither was he asking for permission. He was sleeping here tonight.

"Thanks Max," she said. She appreciated that he had left all he had doing, and came to her. "Let's go

Devi," she said to her puppy, who seemed not to want to go with her, but stay with Max. "Devi!" she said louder, earning a chuckle from Max.

Catherine didn't go to bed immediately. Her room light off, she sat on the floor in her closet, staring at the black envelope. To open or not to open it, that was the question. She sighed as with one move, she reached for it. The envelope was sealed, and she carefully opened it, reaching inside and pulling out three passports. Her eyes narrowed as she flipped them open. What on earth!

The data pages of each of the passport had Megan's face. Well, one of them had her with ugly bangs, the other with some bulky reading glasses, and the other in a curly wig, but they were all Megan's face. But the names, date of births, and other information was different. Alexis Button? Sofia Santiago? Naomi Steffon? And why was she registered as an Italian citizen in one of the passports? She kept staring at the passports. It just didn't make any sense. Why would her friend have passports with different identities? Were they fake? Or was Megan involved in some clandestine deal?

The envelope still had more contents. A metal flash drive, a flip mobile phone which was off, and a single key.

She tried turning the phone on, but the battery had to be dead, and she didn't have a charger for it. She got her laptop from her room, and returned to the closet, sliding the drive into the slot.

It was encrypted which wasn't a surprise. She typed in Megan's birthday, but it was incorrect, with a warning: four more tries. Her eyes narrowed, what was going to happen if the tries were exhausted? Was it going to blow up or something? She groaned in frustration as she removed the drive.

What on earth was going on here? The passports, drive, key, and phone. She was worried about what Megan had been involved in. There had to be a valid reason for everything. Right? Because none of it made sense!

She climbed into bed, deciding that she needed some rest, at least a clarity of mind to think about all that was going on. However, she could not sleep, she kept on turning and tossing, and even Devi could not sleep as well, probably disturbed by her insomnia.

Catherine was up early the following morning. Max was already up, taking a cup of coffee, and on his laptop. "I made you coffee," he said, nodding at the coffee maker.

"I am going for a run. Need to clear my head," she said. She was already dressed in a matching running outfit, and sneakers.

"I am coming with you," Max said.

She gave him a look. "You don't need to. It's not like those guys from last night are going to pull over in a van, and push me in," she said with a chuckle. But this morning Max had no sense of humor, frowning at her.

"I am coming with you," he insisted.

He ran behind her, almost catching up with her. The police officer had suggested going with them, but Max had told him to stay behind and look after the house. "Best not to leave it along for anyone to come in," he had said.

About an hour later, she returned home, feeling alive, with the blood pumping through her veins. She made a fresh cup of coffee, and had one, before heading into the bathroom for a bath. There was a knock on the door just as she stepped out of the bathroom. She opened it, realizing as she did that she had nothing on but her towel.

"Oh!" Max said, his eyes raking over her. "I'm sorry, I didn't know you were…"

She chuckled. Was he actually shy? "It's not like you haven't seen everything before," she could not help but tease.

His face grew redder. "Umm… I am going to go."

Really? Before he could leave, she pulled him to herself, planting a kiss on his lips. Damn, she had missed his taste….

She had no idea how long they laid here, but it felt like the most comfortable place in the world, just being next to him, she could afford to let go of her worries and fears. She heard him get out of the bed, and her eyes opened as she stared at him. It was sad to see him put on his clothes. Why couldn't they lie in bed naked, just having a good time?

"We need to talk," Max said.

When you get dressed," he said firmly.

She rolled her eyes. She had an inkling about what they wanted to talk about. Yes, they needed to talk about whatever was going on between the both of them. Once could be termed a mistake, but after this morning, there was no doubt that there was something hot brewing between them.

Tehila was making breakfast when she got downstairs. The woman ran to her, burying her with a hug. "I am so sorry! I came as soon as Max called me. This is all my fault. If I hadn't—"

"Don't do that Tehila. You have nothing to do with this. Nothing!" Catherine scolded her. It occurred to her right then that things may have gone south if

Tehila was around. What if she had stumbled upon them, and they had hurt her? It was better she had not been around.

"But how did they know you were not going to be alone?" Tehila asked.

It was the same question Catherine asked herself since last night. They had known too much, about the side gate, Tehila's absence, where the bags were kept, way too much that it made her question a lot.

"The police are on it. I am hoping they can give us the answers," Catherine said.

"Well, I have made breakfast. And you have to eat everything, after all that happened yesterday," Tehila said.

Catherine realized she was quite hungry as she ate every last bit of breakfast. She didn't protest when Tehila added some egg to her plate. She had been hungrier than she realized.

"So, you wanted to talk about something," Catherine said, joining Max at the patio.

"About Singapore," he nodded. "And this morning. I apologize if I treated you wrongly," he continued.

She lifted a brow.

"I usually don't get involved with my clients. I admire you a lot Catherine, and hold you in high esteem, I—"

"Nothing happened that I did not want Max. Stop treating me like I am a fragile doll. I am a grown woman who acted on my feelings," she pointed out.

"You were in a vulnerable place back in Singapore," he said.

Catherine sighed. Did he really want to do this? "Max, I had sex with you because I wanted it. Let's be clear on that. It would have happened sooner or later," she added with a shrug.

He lifted a brow, and she nodded. She realized it was bound to happen, and that Megan's death had just been the catalyst.

"You are pretty sure of yourself," he pointed out, with a growing smirk.

She smiled. "Let's not act like you haven't been ogling me in the past," she teased. It was a joke, but the way his face turned red, she knew she was right on the target. So Megan had been right all this while, he had liked her. How could she have been so blind to see what was right in front of her?

"I respect you a lot Cathie. You are one of the smartest and most hardworking women I know," he began.

"Max, I respect you as well, but I can see the wheels turning in your head. I am not asking for a ring. I don't want commitment. Heck, I haven't even had the time to figure out what is going on between us. Let's not worry about it now, please? Let's just go with the tide and not destroy what we have?" If a sexual relationship was going to get in the way of the professional and platonic relationship they had going on, then she wanted no part of it.

He looked like he wanted to say something, but he decided otherwise. "So what's your plan for today?" he asked.

"Meeting with Don. He has a lot of questions about Megan. I don't even know what to tell him," she said with a sigh.

"Just tell him investigations are ongoing."

"What if her body is never found?" Catherine asked. They needed closure, and needed to put her friend to rest by properly burying her, with a headrest that shoved she was loved, and missed by those she had left behind. She would always be haunted if they never found Megan's body.

"We will find her, and I promise we will bring her home for a proper funeral," Max promised with such a conviction she was scared for a moment.

He offered to follow her to the office, but she turned him down, telling him she will be all right. He had to have a lot to do, and she didn't want him to babysit her.

The cop came in to let her know he was leaving, and generous Tehila had offered him breakfast he couldn't resist. He was going to be back later in the night, he said excitedly.

As she headed to work, Catherine had a whole lot on her mind. What she had found about Megan intrigued her, and she needed answers. Ten minutes to her office, she did a turn on the road, headed downtown.

Megan lived in a quiet condo apartment building. She was one of the first tenants to move in about four years ago when it was listed. She liked it because of how quiet it was. "No noisy neighbors. Everyone goes to work, or stays out of each other's business. I don't even get a hello in the elevator," she had said, pretty much pleased when Catherine had pointed out that living in such a place would probably drive her nuts. While Catherine liked quiet, she also liked company. She always interacted with her neighbors, inviting them over. Too bad, her new neighbors who had moved in last year were stuck-up, so she didn't bother.

There was a familiar-looking security guard at the front desk, playing solitaire on the desktop. He absently waved her off, and she glared at him as she walked past him. So he had not noticed that Megan had not been home for weeks? But then, she couldn't blame him.

Whenever she was around, she was indoors attending online meetings, or she was either out of town, going for work meetings. But with what she had found, she could not help but wonder what meetings Megan had really been attending.

The door had a two-way security system. Keys and a security alarm system. Catherine put in the password which Megan had shared with her, then reached for the bundle of keys she always kept with her. Megan had also kept a spare with her, in case anything goes wrong, Catherine frowned as she recalled her saying in the past. What had she meant by that? The need to use the key had never risen, until now.

The living room was dark as she stepped in, and so was the rest of the house, as Megan had shut down her power. She switched on her phone's torch and made her way to the power box, then flipped it on.

It was a cozy apartment; Megan was not big on design, but she was on comfort, ensuring that whatever she brought into her home not only served a purpose but was also comfortable. She had a thing for the antique, and had visited several antique shops in Florida to pick up select items, like her bed that came with a bedpost.

Megan stood in the living room, staring around. No picture frames, nothing, to even suggest that this was Megan's home. It was just empty.

The kitchen was the liveliest place in the home, and that was because Megan liked to cook. Despite how busy she was, she made out time to cook. She called it her safe place, alluding it to her grandmother who was an amazing cook.

Pots and pans were neatly arranged on the cabinet tops. She opened the fridge and wasn't surprised to find it empty, since Megan had cleared everything out before going to Cannes.

The next stop was her room. She stood in the doorway, pushing back tears. How many times had she been in this very room talking and laughing with Megan while they tried on what Megan was going to wear on their girl's hangout. Or the gossip they exchanged about the few people they knew in common. She was definitely going to miss her!

She had no idea what she was looking for, but something out of the ordinary she suspected. She opened the closet and went through it. Clothes, shoes, bags, a couple of other things, and that was it… she groaned in frustration as she stepped out of the closet.

What on earth was she even looking for? At least some pointers would help huh?

She huffed as she tried to remove the mattress from the bed, but it was too heavy, and wouldn't budge with her strength. She gave up on it in frustration. The bathroom was next. Megan hated shower stalls, and had installed a claw tub. She opened her drug closet above the sink. A couple of pills, condoms, lotion, and that was it.

Her phone rang. It was Dave, Megan's brother calling.

"Oh, hi Dave," she said, calming her breath.

"Catherine, can we meet?" he asked.

"Oh yeah, sure, I am currently at Megan's place, but we can meet at the Starbucks close to her place in…" she stared at her wristwatch. "An hour?"

"That's fine with me," he said.

It seemed there was nothing here, or she was just not looking in the right places. She closed her eyes and allowed herself to be calm. She knew Megan well, at least she believed she knew her well enough. Where would her friend hide something, that others wouldn't easily stumble upon? Megan would keep it in plain sight, somewhere easily used, it would be staring at you just right in your face.

The kitchen! Catherine returned this kitchen. As she looked around from the doorway, she had a different view of it. Questioningly. Curious. And determined.

She flipped open the cabinets, ransacking through the contents. There was nothing! At least what she seemed to be looking for.

"Arrrrghhhhh!!" she kicked the island in frustration. She yelped at the pain as she looked up, to the ceiling. Her eyes narrowed as she stared up at a vent. She hurried up the island, reaching for the vent cover. It was screwed closed, but that did not stop her. She pulled out a toolbox from under the kitchen sink and focused on the bolts of the vent with a screwdriver. It didn't even take her a minute, as the bolts were loose on the vent, recently used she thought as she raced in excitement. The cover made a grating sound as she removed it. She stretched out her hand into the darkness. She almost missed it, the lapels of a bag. She reached for it, pulling it to herself.

It was a black beaten-up duffel bag. Heavier than she expected as she dropped it on the table with a lump. What was she going to find in there? She thought excitedly.

Her mouth dropped open as she zipped the bag open. "Holy shit!" she whispered, throwing frantic looks around, despite being alone. "Holy shit!" she repeated.

Guns! There were guns in the bags. And this were not props. They were fucking real! And she knew it because she had used a gun at the shooting range before. She pulled out a revolver, it was sleek and pretty. She opened the magazine, there were bullets inside.

Her hands shook as she pulled out a rifle. As she stared at it, she knew this was no ordinary rifle. She took a picture of it, then placed it next to the revolver. There were three other guns, all loaded. And then a host of bullet casings, and… knives… ropes… and some weapons she had no idea what they were, with a set of walkies.

What the fuck had Megan being involved in? It was not prostitution or drug trafficking as she had suspected. This was way more! This was some high-

Her hand felt something metal. She frowned as she pulled it out of the bag. Her eyes widened as she stared at the FBI Badge.

"HOLY SHIT!" She said as the truth unveiled itself. Her darling best friend of over ten years was FBI!!

Catherine drank a glass of scotch from a bottle Megan had. And then another glass, because she damn as hell needed it. The truth was crazy to even accept. Her Megan was an FBI agent? As much as it seemed far-fetched, it all made sense, and everything seemed to fall into place. How Megan's suspicion had always turned out right, it had been her skills kicking in, or perhaps she had just run a background check.

Pride reared its head first. Her friend had all these years been working for the government, and she had not known? How had she been able to play this game for so long, without her having the faintest suspicion? She had to give it to Megan, she had masterfully created an illusion. The pride dissolved into anger. Why had Megan not trusted her with her secret? Of course she would have told no one. Megan had known everything about her, and it hurt her that her friend had not confided such important information with her.

It was unfortunate that she could not scold her friend for keeping such away from her. "I'm proud of you," she said aloud, to the empty room.

Now that the truth was out, she suspected that Megan's kidnap and death was connected to her job as an FBI agent. Sure, there were twisted people out there, but random kidnapping and killing didn't just happen. It all had to be connected!

She stared at the bag for a moment, then made a decision to replace it. All except for Megan's badge which she slipped into her purse. She returned the vent cover, and took a step back, taking in the kitchen, to ensure that she had not disrupted anything. Eventually, she would have to summon up the courage to pack up Megan's things, and donate them to charity. She still had about four months left on her lease, enough time at least Catherine hoped for her to grow the courage.

"Shit!" Catherine cried out as she walked into a broad chest as she walked out the door.

"Are you okay?" It was Megan's brother, Dave.

"Oh, hi Dave, I didn't know you were coming here," Catherine said, flashing a smile at him.

"Yeah, I decided to come by instead. Leaving?" he asked.

She opened the door, sighing as they returned into the gloomy room. There was a heaviness that hung around.

"I am so sorry about Megan," Catherine said, watching him as he circled around the living room, as if taking all of it in.

"What actually happened to her? You didn't give me answers. Where is she?" Dave asked.

"I…" Her phone buzzed. It was Max calling. "Excuse me, I need to take this," Catherine said as she answered the phone. "Hi Max," she said.

"Where are you?" he asked.

She rolled her eyes at his question. So she was supposed to tell him where she was all the time?

"I am at Megan's home," she said.

"What are you doing there Catherine?" he snapped.

"Clearing up her things. And don't worry, I am fine, Dave is with me. Remember her brother?" she flashed a smile at Dave. The men had met once, or was it twice before.

Max sighed. "I have some news for you. Megan's body has been found."

Her hand flew to her mouth and Dave went over to her side in concern. She waved him off, as she pushed her tears back.

"Is she…" Deep down, she had held on to some ray of hope that the picture had been altered and that Megan was still alive.

"I am sorry Catherine, but she's dead," Max said. "It was identified and is being brought into the US. It should be here by nightfall. I just wanted you to know," he said, his tone softer.

She nodded. "I will… I will talk to you later Max."

"Is everything okay?" Dave asked.

She dabbed a tear away. "Yeah, you were asking about Megan. Can we leave here please?" she asked. Being here, especially after the news Max had just given her made her feel all choked up from the inside.

She made her way past him out of the apartment, her hands shaking as she locked the door. She didn't look back, hurrying down the hallway. It was only when they emerged out of the apartment building that she was able to breathe properly.

The Starbucks was a bit empty when they got there, and she made her way to a table at the end of the room. A waiter was by their side in no time, and she ordered for a cappuccino.

"A caramel coffee, black," he said.

"Megan and I went to Cannes a couple of weeks ago. For a holiday. I was working, and she was supposed to have some time to rest. One morning, I got a message to meet up with the client. When I returned, she was gone." It still seemed surreal every time she narrated what had happened. All it had taken was one moment. A moment for her to leave the house, and Megan had been killed.

"That is dreadful! Megan was kindhearted and peaceful. She would never hurt anyone. Do the police know who did this?" Dave asked.

She could imagine the pain he was going through. It had been him and Megan since foster home. Them against the world, as Megan liked to say. She reached over, placing her hand over his comfortingly.

"They are still investigating. But I know they are going to find the bastard. Even if it is going to take them five years to do it, they will find him. I know the consulate are working on this as well, it is just a matter of time," Catherine said.

"Thank you," Dave flashed a weak smile. "I still can't believe that's she gone. I…"

"Do you know if she had any enemies?" Catherine asked.

Dave frowned in confusion, and she wished she hadn't asked the question. "What do you mean? Wasn't it a random person who killed her?"

"I… I don't think so. I think it is someone she knew. I don't even know what's going on," she said. She was sure that he knew nothing about Megan being a federal agent. If Megan hadn't told her, then certainly she hadn't told Dave. "Her body has been found and she's being brought over. You are her family, and I suppose you would like to help with the funeral," she said. She may have been closer to Megan, but Dave was first her family and his opinion played an important role.

He nodded. "Of course. Just keep me updated please," he said, taking a sip from his coffee.

"Knowing Megan, she would have wanted a simple funeral that wouldn't hazzle anyone. I should probably check if she made any arrangements for that," Catherine said, more to herself. She would have to call Megan's lawyer, Mr. Gray, a quiet older man, Catherine had met a couple of months ago when she went over to Megan's place. He had been leaving, while she came in, and Megan had introduced them briefly.

"Why did you invite your lawyer over? Getting me out of the will?" Catherine had teased. She had expected Megan to laugh but she hadn't, putting up a straight face instead.

She left Dave at the Starbucks with a promise to keep him updated with all that was going on. She didn't feel like going to work, but she needed all the distraction, and in a couple of minutes she pulled into the car park of her office.

There were a couple of customers being attended to. She exchanged pleasantries with them, and even took a picture or two, before heading to her office. She settled in and did a google search of Thomas Gray law firm. It popped up immediately which was a relief. She found his number on the law firm's website and called it.

"Good afternoon, I don't think you remember me, this is Catherine, Megan's friend. We met a couple of months ago at her apartment," she said.

"I do remember you Catherine," the man said in a firm voice.

"I have terrible news. Megan is dead," she said.

"My condolences," he said.

She lifted a brow. He didn't sound surprised. Was that normal in his line of work, she wondered? Or perhaps he just didn't have an intimate relationship with Megan. She was lost in her thoughts she didn't realize he was talking to her.

"Are you still there miss?" he called.

"Oh yes! Sorry. You were saying?" she asked.

"I enquired about the circumstances regarding her death," Thomas Gray asked.

"She was murdered while we were on a trip in Cannes," Catherine said.

"I see. Megan made arrangements for her funeral while she was alive. It was her wish that she be cremated, with her ashes given to you. She said you would know what best to do with it."

Catherine was crying quietly at his words. Oh Megan! They hadn't had much conversations about death, because it terrified Catherine after losing her grandparents so soon after the other, but she recalled one question where Megan had stated that she did not want to be stuck in the earth with some lame ass headstone. Instead, she preferred being cremated, with her ashes scattered over the Red Sea. She had visited Egypt and had fallen in love with the country.

"She set aside a fund for her funeral, so when necessary, kindly provide me with the relevant details," the lawyer was saying. "Also, she had a will, and gave instructions that it should be read within five days after notice has been given of her death."

It all seemed so mechanic, with the way Megan had prepared for the great beyond that Catherine could not help but ask, "Is this normal with your clients? You know what, never mind," she said.

"Megan was particular in ensuring her estate and affairs were settled. She was realistic, knowing that death would eventually come, as it does for all man," the lawyer said. "I suggest we have the will reading in two days. It is nothing elaborate, there will be a notary public available, and you of course," he continued.

She burst into tears when the call was over. Her throat felt lumpy, and the tears just kept on falling and falling. She missed her friend so freaking much, and hated that all of this was going on. Why couldn't she be around for a couple of more years? For them to grow old and gray? Why did this have to happen.

It took a couple of minutes for her to compose herself. She must look a mess she thought as she reached into her bag for her makeup. Her hand touched something hard and she removed it. It was Megan's FBI badge. She stared at it intensely. Knowing that Megan was a federal agent definitely changed things, but she had no idea where to go from here.

CHAPTER 13

THE CONSULATE WAS busy when Catherine arrived. She had to wait for about twenty minutes before she was attended to.

"I want to see Frances Burkle, or Nelson Peters," she said. The woman behind the counter frowned in confusion.

"We don't have anyone by those names who work here," the woman said.

It was Catherine's turn to be confused. She laughed awkwardly. "You are joking right. I saw them here," she pointed towards the office they had sat for the interview.

"I have been working here for five years, and I know everyone that works here ma'am," the woman said confidently.

"Well, let me speak to your bosses, I am sure they know who I am talking about," Catherine said.

"Do you have an appointment?'

Catherine scoffed. "Seriously?"

The woman nodded. "You need to have an appointment to speak to my superiors," the woman flashed a smile at her.

Catherine fumed as she returned to her car. Why on earth did the woman refuse her to see her colleagues? A better question, why would she lie? Her eyes narrowed. What if the woman was being truthful? That only meant one thing, Frances and Nelson were not who they said they were. She gulped at the realization. Then who the hell were they? And why would they lie about their identities? She reached for her phone to call Max but decided otherwise.

About thirty minutes later, Catherine pulled up in front of the FBI office in Jacksonville. Well, not exactly pulled up. She needed security clearance to get in, and since she had none, she flashed Megan's badge at the security.

"I need to speak to Frances Burke or Nelson Peters. Tell them it is important," she said fiercely.

For a moment, she thought she was going to be kept waiting, but a couple of minutes later, the gate opened and she was let into the compound. It was her first time in a federal agency like this, and her heart raced in excitement.

She parked in an empty space, and when she got down, a security guard was waiting for her. He searched her, and satisfied she was carrying no weapons, said, "Come with me please." He handed her a visitors badge then led her into the main building. She kept looking around as they walked down hallways, wondering if she would see someone she knew.

"Wait here," he said, opening a door into a small interview room. "Someone will be with you shortly."

She looked around as she stepped into the room. It reminded her of the ones in movies, and she could bet that she was being watched from the one-sided window that occupied a wall. She waved at whoever was on the other end. Yeah, she knew she was being watched, she thought as she settled into a steel chair.

A couple of minutes later, the door opened. She was not surprised to see both Frances and Nelson. She did a little jump of victory inside. She had been right!

"You can wipe the smug look off your face," Nelson said as he sat opposite her.

"You both lied to my friend and I. You were not consulate, you were FBI!" she glared at them.

"Who we are is none of your business. What matters is that we are working to find your friend's murderer. You shouldn't have gone through all this trouble to prove a point," Frances said. "How did you even—"

Catherine slammed the badge on the table. The agents exchanged a worried look.

"Where did you get this from?" Nelson asked. He tried to reach for it, but Catherine pulled it back.

"How I got it is none of your business. But I know that Megan was one of you. She was a federal agent, and I need answers, because you both are not being truthful with me," Catherine said.

"Yes, your friend was one of ours, but as you know, federal dealings are not for the ears of civilians. It would do you well to steer clear of this," Nelson snapped.

Catherine glared right at him. "Are you threatening me?"

"No, he's not," Frances said quietly, throwing her colleague a warning look. "What we are saying is that this is being investigated, and it is advisable that you don't interfere in the matter. Megan was one of us, she was a valuable officer, and we will find her killer."

Catherine scoffed. "Clearly not enough is being done, because I was attacked yesterday in my home!"

She frowned at their reactions. Or better still, lack of it. They didn't seem surprised about the attack, which meant one thing…

"Did you have someone come into my home last night?" she asked with a glare.

"Hell no! Why on earth would we do that?" Nelson glared back at her.

"All we need is a badge and order and we will search your home," Frances added. "We understand that you were attacked, and we apologize for the inconvenience but—"

"The person that killed Megan is the one behind the attack right?" she asked.

The officers exchanged a look. "We cannot be certain right now, but we suspect so, and this is why we want you to be careful and not interfere with our investigation. The less you know, the better," Frances advised.

"Again, did she give you anything? Megan I mean, like a dossier, a drive? Anything?" Nelson asked.

"No, she did not. Why would she? I didn't even know she was a federal agent," Catherine pointed out.

"Let us know if you do find something. It could help us with finding her killer," Frances said, handing her a card.

Standing outside the door was the guard from earlier. He led her out to her car… She froze in front of her car. Fuming by her car was the last person she expected to see.

"Give me your car keys!" Max snapped.

"What the hell do you think you were doing?" Max yelled. She had never seen him this mad before. The ride to her home had been bloody quiet. She had sensed his anger, and had not even bothered telling him she wasn't done working for the day.

One look at his face and Tehila had scurried off with her tray of cookies. Even Devi was nowhere to be found. The bloody traitor!

"I am not a child that you can shout at!" Catherine glared.

"Then stop acting like one!" he threw back at her.

"What were you doing there?" she asked, folding her arms across her chest. How had he known she was there? She had not told him, so how?

"How I know where you were is not what of relevance now," he scolded.

"It is! Do you know Frances and Nelson are FBI agents?" He didn't look surprised at the news. "Of course, you knew!" She took a moment to gather her feelings and then… "Which means you knew all this while that Megan was a federal agent?" Oh shit! He knew as well from that blank look on his face. Oh shit! She was the only one who was in the dark. "How… how did you know and I didn't?" she asked, more to herself than him. "How did you know?" she yelled.

"Because I am FBI too," he said quietly.

Her mouth dropped open. Like fucking dropped open as she stared at him in wonderment. Hell freaking no! He had not just said that! Nope, he was just kidding around? Right? But he looked damn serious.

She giggled, and it grew into a full-blown laughter. "You are joking right?" she said.

"What do you think?" he asked, folding his broad arms.

"I don't know what to think! I don't know! But it just doesn't… it doesn't make sense!" she cried in frustration.

"I am sorry that you had to find out this way, about Megan, and about me, but being a federal agent means our identities are kept hidden," Max explained.

"Not from your friend! Not from someone you have screwed! It never occurred to you all these years to tell me who you really are? Or for Megan to confide in me huh?" she snapped.

"You have every right to be angry," he said, attempting to pull her into a hug, but she slapped his hand off, moving away from him. She sat on the bed, staring at a spot on the window, with a glimpse of outside.

"I'm sorry Megan," he said, sitting next to her.

"How?" she asked quietly.

"It was probably college for Megan. College students are young, vibrant and eager to be a part of something big. For me, I got recruited when I returned from my last tour in Afghanistan. I knew I could not return to a normal life, and it just seemed like the good thing to do at that time," Max said.

"But you are a manager, in entertainment industry," she pointed out.

"In name actually. Around the time we met, we had a security threat, a Russian actress…"

"Mena," Catherine said quietly. He nodded. Mena had been a bigshot Russian actress who had stormed Hollywood. She had been alleged to be the daughter of a heiress and had thrown wild luxurious parties, a couple of which Catherine had attended.

"We had intel she was working for the KGB, and we needed someone who could infiltrate. I was supposed to be a part of her security detail, but we soon found out it was a much bigger cell than expected. We needed someone who could fit into the industry as an everyday life. Your manager at the time had quit, and I was having a tough time as well, so I came to you."

"What happened to her?" Catherine asked.

The actress' suicide had come as a shock to many, as she had been considered vibrant and full of life. She had left behind a note, stating she was depressed, but with what Max had said, he suspected otherwise.

"Let's just say it was taken care of by the FBI to safeguard our national security," Max said. "And after that, it just seemed like a good plan to have a couple of others remain undercover in the industry. We are everywhere, colleges, financial institutions, religious bodies…"

"You used me!" Catherine spat.

"I am not going to deny it Catherine. I did what I had to do, but I have never hurt you, or gotten you involved in any nefarious activity. The FBI knows fully well that you are never to be put in harm's way. Hate me for taking advantage when the opportunity came about, but you cannot deny that I did what I promised when you agreed to be my client."

That she could not deny. Max had delivered marvelous deals to her on a platter of gold since he had become her manager. Even deals she wondered how he had gotten a hold of. Now she knew better, he had his ears on matters many in the industry were not privy to.

"And Megan? Did she know you were using me? Was it her idea?" she asked.

He shook his head. "I didn't even know who Megan was, well I had heard about her. She had a badass reputation at the Bureau. We had heard of each other in passing, but it was not until I was going to be your manager that we got to meet each other," Max smiled sadly.

"What's funny?" Catherine growled.

"She did a background check on me, and it seemed kind of sketchy. She put two and two together and got my file then came to my house one morning and told me we had to talk. She threatened me. Told me if I ever hurt you, or got you in the line of fire, she was going to slit my throat wide open, and watch me bleed," Max said.

That was gory, but it did sound like what Megan would say. She had been quite protective of her.

"So yeah, I knew who she was, and she knew who I was. We both respected that, at least from a distance, but we never worked together. Megan was more... espionage."

"And that got her killed," Catherine said. "Who killed her Max?" He was quiet. "I need to know Max. She was my best friend!"

"We don't know Catherine. She was one of our best field agents. She had been working on a number of cases. She had made enemies in the past. Powerful enemies. It could have been anyone," Max said.

"The man she met in Cannes killed her," Catherine said. "If you guys can find him, then… You know who it was!" She had noticed the grimace he made when she mentioned the man Megan met.

"Yes we do. He's a rogue agent. They were lovers, but I don't think he killed her. Kirk cuts corners, he does whatever he pleases to get the work done, and has been suspended more times than I can count, but he wouldn't kill her."

"Then he knew who killed her. You guys need to find him," Catherine said.

"Oh don't worry, I will, and when I do I am going to kick his ass for giving you those pictures," Max frowned.

"What are you saying?" Catherine wasn't following.

"He wasn't supposed to give you those pictures. He snapped after Megan died and hasn't reported to headquarters since, and the higher ups are worried about what he's going to do," Max explained.

"You already knew Megan was dead when we left for Singapore," Catherine stared at him in anger.

He was quiet, but the answer was clear. All that while, she had been worried about her friend, and he had acted ignorant.

"You knew! Max you knew!" she pointed at him.

"How was I going to tell you when the local police were still looking for her? I am sorry Catherine for keeping the truth from you, but I did it to protect you," Max explained.

"No, you did it to protect yourself," Catherine said, dabbing the tears that were straining to roll down her eyes. She got up and opened the door wide open. "Please leave, I need to be alone," she said quietly.

"Come on Catherine. Please, let's talk about this…" he pleaded.

"Leave Max!" her voice grew louder.

His shoulders relaxed in resignation. He walked to the door and stopped. "Know that I will always be here for you, and I did all I did to protect you. Call me later so we can talk."

She slammed the door behind him then threw herself on the bed and burst into tears. She was mad at him and Megan. Furious at everyone for being deceived and being led along by the people she cared the most

about. She had opened up to them, made herself vulnerable, and they had held back so much, she could not
help but wonder if they had ever been honest with her.
Had their relationship all been make believe?

CHAPTER 14

CATHERINE WAVED OVER to Dave as he got down from his blue Subaru. She chuckled at how nerdish he looked as he hurried over to her wearing a thick jacket and heavy glasses. He was always that way, Megan used to say, his head buried in his books.

"How's the doctorate going?" she asked as they worked into the building that housed the lawyer's office. Dave was currently working on getting a doctorate at some small private school, which was incredibly smart of him. Catherine had tried to get back into college some years ago, but had decided that it was not for her during the first semester.

"I am going to round up in three months," Dave smiled at her.

"Megan would be so proud of you," Catherine said.

They walked into the lobby and met with an older woman, who gave them a suspicious look.

"What do you want?" she asked.

"We are here to see Thomas Gray," Catherine said. She had decided that it was best to invite Dave over for the will reading. He had been her family, and he would be a beneficiary. To be honest, she wasn't expecting much, and she had contemplated telling Dave to go alone. But her anger had relaxed, and she had decided to be there. Despite all that had happened, she loved Megan, like she was her sister.

"I don't think he would be seeing anyone after what happened yesterday," the woman said.

Catherine exchanged a confused look with Dave. "What do you mean?"

"Oh, let them in!" a gruffy voice said from behind them.

It was Thomas Gray, and he was with another man, in the same age bracket, whom she assumed was the notary.

They exchanged pleasantries and Catherine introduced Dave to the men. The lawyer frowned as he stared at Dave, "I see, I was expecting you to come alone however," he said, leading the way down a dimly lit hallway.

"What happened yesterday? The woman out front said something happened?" Catherine said.

"There was a break-in last night. Tore my office apart," Thomas Gray said as he fiddled with a pair of keys.

"Were you hurt?" Catherine asked in concern.

"Luckily, I was not in. Received a call that there was a fire at my home. But it was a false alarm," the man said as he opened the door, the others going behind him. But Catherine stayed behind, frozen in her thoughts. A false alarm! Just like in Cannes.

"Who was the person who called? A neighbor?" she asked, as she stepped into the chaos of the outer room. It was a small waiting room and the couch had been ripped apart. Books were piled on a desk, and she suspected that they had occupied the shelf before the break-in.

"I have no idea. It came from a random number which was turned off when I called back. You should see the inside, I don't know how I am going to deal with it. Tony," he nodded at the notary. "Suggested we do this some other time, but I would rather respect the dead last wishes."

"Did they take anything?" Catherine asked.

He shook his head. "I keep nothing of value here. All the wills and codicils are kept at a safe in a bank," the man chuckled with confidence. "All they did was waste their time and resources."

"Are you okay?" Catherine asked Dave as he glared around.

"Just wondering who would do such a terrible thing," Dave said.

She had an idea who it was, but she would rather not divulge the information. This made her realize how Megan and Max must have felt, knowing something, but unable to share because of how sensitive it was. If she had been in their place, she would have done same.

"Maybe we should return tomorrow," Catherine suggested. It just did not seem like a good time to go ahead with the will reading.

"I insist we do it now, you are here after all," Thomas Gray said.

He opened his briefcase and pulled out a sealed envelope, which he passed around for confirmation that it was sealed. "This is the last will and testament of Megan Sloane," he said loudly, as he unsealed the envelope, pulling out a type-written document. He went on with some legal terms confirming the authenticity of the will.

"To Catherine, my dearest friend and sister, I leave all my assets, not limited to the money in all my bank accounts, both local and foreign, my shares of which certificates will be given to you. The details of every assets owned by me as at the date this will was made are in the appendix attached. Whatever changes have been made also apply, and are effective. I give you everything I have," the lawyer read.

"Oh my!" Catherine gasped as the lawyer handed her the appendix. Holy shit! Megan had over two million dollars in her asset. She had known she had some money, but this much. Oh Megan! She fought the tears back, not wanting to make a baby of herself in front of these men. Dave!

"I'm so sorry Dave. I… thought there was something in there for you," she said as it dawned on her he had been left out of the will. "Didn't she give anything to Dave?" she asked the lawyer.

"I am sorry, everything goes to you," Thomas Gray said.

"I should go," Dave said getting up. He looked really hurt with a fallen face. How embarrassing this had to be for him. She went after him as he hurried out.

The lawyer called out to her. "We still have a lot, as she left behind a letter for you!"

"I will be right back!" she called back to him, meeting up with Dave. "I had no idea she left nothing for you Dave. It would be cruel of me not to give you anything. She was your family. Why don't we meet later in the week to talk things out," she said, with a kind smile.

"You don't have to do anything Catherine. I am doing okay, I always have. Just keep me updated about the cremation. I would like to say one last goodbye to her," Dave said.

She watched him walk away with guilt. She felt bad that she got to inherit everything, while he got nothing. She had thought their relationship was actually great, but Megan was not the type of person to spite others. She had to have had a good reason to exclude him out of her will. Had they had a fight? She tried to recall any conversation about Dave in the past months, but she couldn't. The last time she had asked about him, Megan had told her he was doing great and had changed the subject.

The lawyer handed her an envelope when she returned to the office. It was dated six months ago, and she figured it had been written the day she had come around when the lawyer had come over.

"She was really fond of you, and again I extend my condolences," Thomas Gray said with a tender smile.

"Thank you," she said. As she headed back home, she realized that a heavy weight seemed to have been lifted off her shoulder. It felt like… she had found peace in some sort of way. She had no idea what was going to be inside the letter, but reading Megan's words were going to give her peace, which she had been—

Catherine screamed as something hit her from behind. It was a truck with tinted glasses. Was he nuts or something? She slowed down for him to drive by since he clearly was in a hurry to get to his destination. Her eyes narrowed as he bumped into her again, this time harder than before. She gulped as he revved away, then bumped harder into her car. Her car spiraled at the force, to a stop.

It was a lone road, with a couple of cars going by. The truck revved, the lights coming alive. She knew without a doubt what it was going to do. This was not random she realized as the car headed towards her with impact in mind. She pressed hard on the break, reversing right into a lamp post that activated her airbag just as her head was about to hit the steering. But that didn't prevent the searing pain in her arm.

The truck stopped right in front of her. She struggled hard with the seat belt, to get out of there. The truck door opened and through flickering eyes she saw a pair of boots.

Bright light made Catherine groan in pain. She tried to lift her hand to cover her eyes but they ached. What was—

"Catherine, you are safe," a familiar voice said.

She turned over to the side and stared right at Max's face. He looked like shit, his eyes bloodshot with an overnight beard.

"Hey…" she said drowsily. "Whereeeeee am I?" Her eyes widened open as she tried to take in her environment. An EKG machine was next to her and… was that an IV line? Why was she in the hospital?

"You need to get some rest. I am here with you my love," Max said, kissing her forehead.

Her eyes drifted close as she was lured into the comfort of his touch and assurance.

The next time she woke up, she was more alert. Yes, she was in the hospital, with Max watching over her. The doctor and nurse had come in to check on her.

"I have a crazy headache," she told them.

"Thankfully, the airbag prevented damage. There's a bit of concussion but a couple of painkillers should clear the pain," the doctor said, writing a prescription.

"What happened?" Catherine asked Max. The last thing she could recall was the crash. And then something… There was something she was supposed to remember, but she couldn't remember.

"You crashed into a lamppost while you were heading back home from the lawyer's," Max said.

"There was a truck, it rammed into me a couple of times, I tried to reverse and drive off, but I wrongly calculated and the lamppost got in my way," Catherine recalled.

Max scowled. "A truck? Describe it!"

"Black truck, tinted windows…" She squinted, the headache hitting harder as she tried to recall. "There were no plates. Yes, there was none," she remembered.

Max typed hard on his phone as he sent a text. "Your car is at the mechanic's. I figured there was more with the dents. It should be out in a couple of days. Did you see who it was?" he asked with concern.

She shook her head. "Just his boots…" The boots, that was what she was trying to remember. There was something familiar about them but she couldn't recall what it was. "I thought he was going to come for me, but… someone came around right?"

"Yes, a delivery truck driver found you soon after the crash. The truck must have left immediately he saw someone else. I am so glad you are all right. I was so worried. Scared. When I got the call," Max said, taking her hand in his.

She could see tears in his eyes, and her heart ached. She had treated him wrongly when all he had been trying to do was protect her. "I'm sorry Max, for being such an asshole," she apologized.

"There's no need to apologize. We should have told you. I should have," he said. "I am not going to let anything happen to you Catherine. I made that promise to myself a long time ago, and to Megan, that I would always protect you. We are going to get this bastard. Fucking get him!" he said with determination.

"Thomas Gray, Megan's lawyer, his office was broken into last night. He was told there was a fire in his home to get him out of the house while he was working late. Same thing that was did to me back in Cannes. I think the person is looking for something," Catherine said.

"We are going to follow that up." Max said, as he sent another text out.

"What really is going on Max? What is he looking for? Nelson asked if Megan left anything behind? What is it?" Catherine asked.

Max sighed, looking at her for a moment as if deliberating if to tell her or not.

"You know what, don't worry, it is none of my business," Catherine waved it off. If it required him breaking his allegiance to the government, then he could keep it to himself.

"Megan was working on something before she died. She found out that some Americans were working for a Mexican cartel, smuggling cocaine into the US. The last time she spoke to the agency, she told them she had a list and was going to get it across when she returned from Cannes."

"She never returned," Catherine said quietly.

Max nodded.

"So, you guys think someone on that list killed her to silence her?" Catherine asked.

"We believe so, but then it could have been someone else, but that is our suspicion for now."

The door flew open and Tehila burst in, hurrying to her side. "Oh, my dear! Look at you! Oh, we thank the heavens that you are alive! I thought my heart was going to give way when Max told me you were in an accident!"

Catherine giggled at how dramatic the woman was. She removed a bowl of meal from her bag, and then another, spreading them on the table. "People these days don't know to drive. It is the automatic stick

I tell you. Has them have so much confidence that they don't know what they are doing. In my time we drove with the manual stick, and we turned out to be the best drivers!"

Catherine exchanged a look with Max who held back a grin. They both knew how much of a terrible driver Tehila was. One time, Catherine had thought she was going to puke in the passenger's seat. It was the last time she had allowed Tehila drive her.

"How are you feeling? When did the doctor say you are coming home?" Tehila asked.

"I feel terrible, like I was in an accident," Catherine said with a chuckle. "I think I should be back home today right?" she directed at Max.

"I don't think you should go home. You will be safer at my place," Max said.

Tehila frowned, confused by what he meant. She waved the older woman off before she worried and asked more questions. "I'm not going to hide in your place Max, I have a home," Catherine refused.

"Which isn't safe. I need my eyes on you all the time, it is the only way I will feel assured," Max said stubbornly.

She was about to rebut him when Tehila interfered. "I don't know what's going on, but I think Max is right.

You need a strong and brave man to look after you." Catherine rolled her eyes at her, making the woman chuckle.

"Fine, but I need to go home to pack my things," Catherine said.

⬯

"That's a lot!" Max whined as she dropped another duffel bag in front of the other two luggage bags.

"You are the one who invited me to move in with you, and I don't pack light," Catherine shrugged. He pouted and she giggled at how much of a baby he was. She was still unsure about staying with him for a couple of days, but he was of the opinion that her home wasn't safe after the break-in. She felt the same as well, and had taken up the offer of him having some men from a security company owned by a former FBI agent, to come around to upgrade the security system.

"I am ready," Catherine said. Devi barked and she knelt down to hug her dog. Max's apartment had a no pet policy, which meant she couldn't take her with her, but she was going to be just as safe with Tehila. "I am going to miss you girl. Be good for me and Tehila huh?" she said as she caressed her.

Max helped with taking the bags to her Range. She was going to be making use of it only until her car was cleared from the mechanic's.

Max lived in a high-rise apartment building in mid Florida. It was one of those pretty buildings with floor to ceiling windows. She had been around a couple of times.

"Welcome home," Max said as she walked in.

"Have I told you your apartment is…"

"A bachelor's pad, yes you have," Max nodded.

He remembered, she smiled. It was clear that there was no woman's touch here from the dark furniture, to the huge TV that occupied an entire wall. It made her smile, knowing that there were no women, well, romantically in his life.

"Your room is down the hall," Max led her down a well-lit hall that had on both sides superheroes posters. She snickered, earning a glare. "Spiderman is the best hero," he advocated.

"Superman begs to differ," she threw back, earning a deeper scowl. He was a huge Marvel fan, and while she wasn't a superhero enthusiast, she chose DC to tease him.

"This is yours," he opened a door, and she walked right past him. She lifted a brow as she took in the room. A huge bed covered in cotton sheets, with a walk-in closet by the side. Fresh flowers were in a jar next to the bed.

"Were you expecting me?" she asked.

He shrugged. "I was going to suggest you stay here before the accident," he said.

"So full of yourself, aren't you? And if I said no?"

He chuckled, taking a step towards her. She moaned as he wrapped his hands around her waist, pulling her to him. "I was going to tie you up and bring you home with me

"You were in an accident!" he screeched the moment she answered the phone.

"How did you find out?" she asked.

"It is on a gossip blog. One of the nurses sent a video of you being brought in. So many people are calling in, to find out if you are okay? Why did you not let us know?" Henry asked.

"Because I am fine Henry, it is just a scratch," she said. The painkillers had worked, and her head didn't hurt anymore. However, she knew during bath time, those scratches were going to itch crazily.

"What happened Catherine?" It was Natalie.

Her heart welled with the concern from her loved ones and friends. She didn't usually appreciate their care for her, but now she did.

"It was just a little accident like I told Henry, I will see you guys tomorrow huh?" she said, ending the call before they could go on fussing over her.

"I should let you rest for a while, you have had quite an eventful day," Max said.

The door closed behind him, shutting her in the silence. This was different. Being in his home, and she did like it. She reached for her handbag, and her hand found the letter from Megan. She stared at it for a moment, deliberating if to read it or not. To be honest, she was afraid of what she would see in there. In one swift move, she ripped the envelope open.

Hi Cathie,

If you are reading this then I am dead. Which sucks pretty bad, because a part of me hoped we would live for a pretty long time until we were old and grey. But that's how life works, you never expect it. But then, I kind of do. I am guessing by now you know about my big secret. Yeah, that surprised you right?

I know you are mad, but please don't be. You have no idea how much I wanted to tell you. I am hoping you don't get this letter, and that I get to tell you myself about my secret. I know you are curious too. How? Well, long story short, I got recruited while I was in college. It's not the best of jobs, but it pays the bills and have me go around the world.

It has always been my plan to keep you away from that world, and I hope it remains the same. I don't know the circumstances of my death. Who did it? Has the person being caught? In my line of work, I doubt whoever did it has been caught. I have too many enemies to be bothered about who pulled the trigger.

There's so much I want to share with you, but the little you know, the safer for you. But what I do want you to know is that you are the best friend a girl could ever have. I know you like to say that I saved you, but you came into my life when everything seemed to be falling apart. I wish we got to spend way more time together, but I am grateful for what we have. And I know you freaking had no idea I am that loaded. I hope it helps with the business and all. And I sure hope *you give Max a chance. That man lights up when you walk into the room. Make love to him a couple of times and make a decision. Life is too short to be lonely.*

I want you to know that you really mattered to me. I am going to miss you. Heck, I don't know how it is going to be from this side. And you had better miss me too!

Love you girl!

The tears dropped on the paper and she pulled it away before she could ruin it. She broke into a full-blown sob, curling up on the bed as she mourned her best friend and a sisterhood that had mattered so much to her.

She drifted asleep, and when she woke up, it was dark outside. She reached for the letter and stared at Megan's writing, her eyes glazing over the words again. There was something about the letter that bothered her. She didn't know what it was, but there was just something Megan had said that was off.

Aroma of grilled chicken greeted her as she stepped out of her room. Max was cooking, she thought with a smile. She walked to the kitchen, watching him as he prepped dinner, while doing some silly dances.

"You dance terribly," she commented.

He chuckled. "Do you know my folks enrolled me in dancing school when I was a kid? I dropped out after I was given a substitute role for a dance performance. To substitute as a tree," he said with an eyeroll as he poured wine into a glass for her.

She giggled, sighing in content as she took a sip of the wine. It tasted great, fruity with a thing of alcohol.

"What are you making and how can I help?" she asked as she washed her hands in the sink.

"Just sit down and eat. I am almost done," Max said as he handed her a towel to dry her hands.

She ignored him and opened a pot on the cooker. Inside was a tomato sauce brewing. It had a yummy aroma and her stomach growled in delight. She was looking forward to having a plateful in front of her.

Despite his refusals that she should sit her ass down, she went about and set the table. In a couple of minutes, dinner was ready, and her mouth watered as he placed a well grilled piece of chicken on her place, accompanying it with fried rice and the tomato sauce.

"Damn! You are competing with Tehila!" Catherine teased as she ate a couple of spoons. She had no idea he was a great cook.

"My mom was bent on all of her kids learning how to cook," Max said with a sad smile. He had lost his mother five years ago, and she knew it had been really tough on him as they had been pretty close. "How are your siblings doing?" she asked.

Max had two siblings, Helen and Noah, and they were pretty close. Helen was a professor in Washington and Noah was married and living in Alaska with his family.

"Helen is thinking of moving to Florida. Advised her to remain in Washington," Max said with a grimace.

"Come on, it's not that bad here," Catherine said. Max gave her a look and she chuckled. Yeah, Florida was crazy, and it took a while for newcomers to adjust. It was becoming pretty much congested, with house rents and unemployment rates going high. "Do they know… what you do?" she asked.

He nodded. "Yeah, but it took me a couple of years to tell them. but Noah figured what I was doing. I trust them to keep my affairs private, so they tell anyone that I work at a security firm."

"I can't believe I didn't figure it out. With you. And with Megan," Catherine berated herself. Had she been so self-absorbed she had not seen what was right in front of her?

"It has nothing to do with you," Max said. "It is just human nature. You let people see what they need to see."

Yeah, she knew people were good with deceit, but she felt like a bad friend for not even being suspicious. Now that she racked her memories, she realized there had been so many clues and she had been ignorant, blind, or rather selfish. Like the times Megan had returned home with bruises or in a bad shape, and had told her she got mugged or ran into something while on a trip? Come on! How could she have actually fallen for all that? There had been that one time her ribs had been badly bruised and she had to get an X-ray and had been on meds. She had believed that she had fallen while paragliding, despite her refusal to sue the management of the company involved. How could she have been so naïve huh?

"Hey, don't overthink things," Max laid his hand over hers, clearly reading her thoughts.

"I just wish I knew. It would have changed things. Made me appreciate her even more. Understand her, and be there for her. Maybe she would still be alive today. I could have…"

"Don't do that Catherine. It may sound harsh, but I don't think you could have prevented her death.

Megan's line of work was intense. I won't go into the details, but she dealt with terrorists, murderers, and people who wanted to kill her. To do her job, she had to step on toes. She did what she had to do, to protect you. If you had gotten in the way…" He shuddered, and she knew what he had left unsaid. She could have gotten hurt in the process as well.

"There's something I need to show you," Catherine said as dinner rounded up.

Max looked at her curiously as she got up. However, he followed her as she headed to the room. In her room, she opened one of her bags and brought out a smaller tote bag. It contained the items she had found in Megan's box.

Max's eyes widened as she poured out the content on her bed. He immediately reached for the thumb drive and the phone.

"How long have you had these?" he asked, with a scowl.

"Since the night of the attack." His frown deepened and she quickly added, "Here me out. I found them by accident, and I didn't know what to do, or who to trust. So I just kept it to myself."

"We need to get these looked at. Is there anything else you are not telling me?" he asked.

She shook her head. "That's all."

His face relaxed and he gave her a smile. "I need to get to the office for a couple of hours. I will be back soon. There's a security system, and my building is very secured. But still, don't let anyone in. And don't leave without letting me know," he said, as he gave her a quick kiss. Then he was gone.

Catherine scrolled through her phone in boredom. She stumbled on two or three articles of her being involved in an accident. On her social media pages, there were a lot of well-wishes, hoping she recovered. She took a picture and uploaded it with a statement that she was doing fine and couldn't wait to be back on the grind, whatever that was, but she had seen it on someone's post before.

"Arrrghhhhh!" she groaned as she flipped through the channels of the TV. She was bored out of her mind. She went on Netflix, and ten minutes into a movie, she mentally logged out. Her mind was distracted and she couldn't figure out what it was it that needed her attention.

Just as she was about to get up to go to the room, there was a knock on the door. She froze.

"Who's that?" she called.

There was no response on the other end. Her frown deepened. She knew it was not Max. He had a key, and besides, he would not remain silent. Her eyes widened in fear as she heard the person on the other end try to open the lock.

"Hey! What do you think you are doing? I am going to call the cops!" she said as she began to dial 911.

"We need to talk Catherine. About Megan," an unfamiliar male voice said. Her murderer! It was him! She thought, her heart racing fast in fear. She quickly looked around for a weapon as she dialed Max's number. It went to voicemail.

"Max, there's a guy outside the door. He's trying to get in. I don't know how he got pass security," she quickly said. She hurried to the kitchen and grabbed a knife. She was not going down without a fight. She held on tight to the knife as she returned to the door.

"I want to talk about Megan. We… we were in love…"

Catherine's fear subsided at his words. He sounded… broken? Her hand hovered over the door handle.

"I fucking miss her! I miss her so much!" And then he broke into a sob. She could hear his muffled cries from the other side.

"Fuck it," she muttered to herself as she opened the door. It was him! She thought with panic. It was the man from the gala. The one who had given her the note. She hadn't seen much of him, but he looked really in bad shape with bloodshot eyes and an overgrown beard. As he stumbled past her, she winced. It seemed he hadn't had a bath in a day. Or two.

"If you even think of doing anything stupid, know that I am going to hurt you anywhere and everywhere," she said as she waved the knife with what she hoped was a fierce look.

He staggered to a couch and flopped on it with a faraway look. He looked around, and her wary eyes followed him as he went over to a table where a bottle of scotch sat. She grimaced as he drank straight from the bottle. Manners gentleman, she said silently.

"What do you want?" she asked, taking a step towards him. She perched on a couch, watching him warily. She hadn't closed the front door completely, in case she needed to get out or scream her lungs out.

"To find the bastard that killed Megan! And when I do, he's going to wish he was never born. I am going to cut his tongue out while he screams out in pain. Then chop his fucking hands off! And his legs, run them over with a bike while he's tied up!"

Catherine grimaced at the graphic image. She sure as hell didn't pity Megan's murderer. He deserved every bit of the painful death this man had in store for him. "How come I never knew about you?" she wondered aloud. Megan had never hinted that she was in a relationship with someone in the period leading to her death. Or perhaps, once again, she had been oblivious.

"She wanted to tell you. But I insisted we kept things private. Not just for us, but for our job. By now you already know what she did. We worked on a case together and… damn, I thought she was a stuck up before we worked together," he said with a sad laugh. "Her head always held high and she always had an opinion for everything. And then we walked together and… I just fell for her. Hard and flat. It started out as a fling, but… Remember the time you dropped by when she was conducting a training session for a new recruit?"

Catherine nodded. That had been about three months ago. She had dropped by after going to the gym. It had taken Megan about twenty minutes to come to the door and Catherine had been worried. Megan had told her she was conducting some training with some dumb trainee. But it had seemed off as she had been covered in sweat, and her eyes had been darting back and forth. She had had to leave shortly after so she wouldn't distract her.

"I was in the bathroom hiding out," he said with a chuckle. "I should have allowed us go public. Maybe if we did, maybe if we didn't hide our love for each other, she would still be alive."

"What's your name?"

His eyes lifted to hers as he said, "Adam. My name is Adam."

Shit! Adam! Two months ago, Megan had gotten a tattoo. Guess what it was? Adam! Catherine had been curious and had asked why she would get a tattoo with that name.

"First man to be created? I totally dig that," Megan had said with a faraway smile, and then burst into a laugh.

She hadn't thought much of it. Damn! She had really been a terrible friend not to have seen what was right in front of her, Catherine thought. So many signs and clues, but she had been blind.

"She wanted you to know about us, but I was worried that if we went public, something was going to go wrong and ruin what we had. You know we had a fight when she was about to go to France? It involved us going public, and I told her not yet. She was pissed. Thought I wasn't proud of her. Told me I needed to make up my mind about us being together..." She winced as he took a mouthful of the drink.

"You were in Cannes."

He nodded. "Came to get her back. Tried to talk to her to let her see things from my point of view, but she told me her stance remained. That was the last time I spoke to her."

He burst into tears, and her heart broke in pain for him. All this while, she had thought she was the only one mourning Megan. He loved her so much, and she could imagine the regrets he had for not letting her know his feelings about her.

"I'm sorry Adam. I really am. Megan was amazing," Catherine smiled sadly.

"She was the best thing that ever happened to me," Adam said as the tears flowed freely. "It feels like a part of me is gone. I won't get it back. Ever!"

She understood perfectly how it felt. She felt empty since Megan's death, and she was sure that emptiness was something she would never be able to replace.

"I tried calling her that night. But her phone was switched off. Then I knew something was wrong. Heard about a missing woman over the police radio and I just knew it! I knew it! I wanted to reach out. Saw you go into the station," he continued.

That made her shudder. To know that she was being watched. She had not been wrong after all. She had felt it while in France and in Singapore.

"And then Max came around. I reached out to him and he told me to stay put. I knew something was wrong. There was no way she would just go away without letting me know, even if we were fighting. I found her you know…" The tears came again. "I went all out into the woods and looked for her. Couldn't and didn't sleep. I found her dead… I found her dead!" He cried like a baby, the tears rolling down his cheeks unendingly.

Tears welled in Catherine's eyes as she relived the trauma with him. This man had gone through so much for the woman he loved. And she wished somehow he hadn't gone through all of that.

"She was already dead when I found her. The bastard! He tortured her. He… broke her…"

"Why give me the pictures?" Catherine asked.

"I wanted you to know the truth. It is what she would have wanted. Max wasn't going to tell you shit. He's a good fella, but he was going to protect you from the truth. Make some story about her falling off a cliff or something. But you deserved to know the truth about how she died. And I thought maybe you knew something. Maybe she told you something that could lead to her murderer. It wasn't my intention to upset you," Adam said, in a somewhat apology.

"So what do we do now?" Catherine wondered aloud. She was not scared as he stood up. He staggered as he knelt next to her. She flinched at the alcohol on his breath, but was willing to give him some grace. He had been through hell these past weeks.

"I want you to think deeply. Did she tell you anything? You may have forgotten about it. Carefully go through the past weeks. Did she say anything? Do anything strange?" he asked.

"No," Catherine shook her head. She had gone down this road several times. There was nothing Megan had said to her that could have been of help.

"No! You need to remember!" Adam said stubbornly as he grabbed her arms.

"Get the hell away from her!" Max yelled as he burst in through the door. He looked really pissed as his eyes darted from Adam to her.

Catherine quickly pulled away from Adam, standing between the men. "It is okay Max, he's just trying to find out who killed Megan," Catherine said. That only seemed to piss Max.

"Adam! You have been told to leave the investigation! We are going to find out who killed Megan, but you need to stay put!"

"You expect me to do nothing? Would you sit your ass down and do nothing if she was hurt?" he snapped, pointing at Catherine.

"Don't bring her into this!" Max rebutted.

"We need to calm down gentlemen," Catherine said, as both men fumed at each other. "Fighting is not going to help anyone," she continued.

"You need to go Adam. You have disrespected me by coming here when I told you to leave Catherine out of this," Max said.

"She needs to know what happened! Megan loved her!" Adam said.

An idea just occurred to Catherine and she glared at Adam. "I saw you at the gala. Were you the one who sent me a message at the airport taunting me?"

Just as she said it, Max lunged at Adam who was not as drunk as she had thought the way he stepped out of the way.

"I am going to kill you!" Max snapped.

"I didn't send her any freaking message!" Adam said.

She didn't know whether to believe him, but why would he lie?

"Calm down!!" Catherine yelled at the top of her voice. The room went quiet as both men fumed at each other. "There's no reason to act like three-year-olds," she scolded. It was time for the both of them to put aside their egos. "What we need to do is find out who killed Megan," she continued.

Adam nodded. "Look I didn't send a message to you. Did I give you a note at Tokyo? Yes, because I needed to have a moment to let you know the truth, because he was hiding it from you. But I would never send you a message taunting you. And yeah, you are right. What we need to do right now is get Megan's killer, and you can help me."

"No, she is not getting involved in this. Megan's death is being investigated," Max pointed out.

Adam scoffed. "You bloody well know the Agency will throw this under!"

"Megan was an asset!"

"And she knew too much. She did too much. All they want to do right now is cover their asses, and if that means ruling her death a suicide or an accident, or just leaving it like that, they will do so!" Adam threw back at him.

Max was quiet, and this made Catherine worried. Would they actually do that? Just act as if Megan hadn't been murdered.

"They wouldn't do that, would they?" she whispered.

"They can, and have done so in the past. No one is indispensable," Adam said.

"So what do we do?" Catherine wondered aloud.

"I don't want you involved in this," Max said, worriedly.

"I am going to be fine Max," Catherine reassured him. "But we need to find out who this person is, or who they are. Whether we like it or not, I am now involved. He know who I am, he has been in my home. He tried to kill me! I won't be able to live normally, without being scared and looking over my shoulder." How long would he continue to watch over her? What of the days he couldn't? She couldn't continue to live her life in hiding. This sick asshole had to be gotten and made to do time.

"Why do you have to be so bloody stubborn?" Max asked, caressing her face.

She stared into his eyes and smiled. She had no response for that, but standing so close to him, being around him made her heartbeat in excitement and she…

Adam cleared his throat and they both glared at him in unison.

"You can save all of that for the bedroom later guys," he said.

He was right. They had all the time in the world for that. "What was on the drive?" she asked.

"What drive?" Adam asked.

Max glared at her, and her face turned red. She hadn't realized she wasn't supposed to ask about the drive. But then, hadn't they agreed they were in this together?

CHAPTER 15

"WHAT DRIVE?" ADAM asked, throwing Max a questioning look.

"It is none…" Max sighed. He walked over to the bar and got himself a glass of whiskey. "This is between you and I you understand?"

Adam nodded.

"Catherine found a flash amongst Megan things. I took it to the Bureau a couple of hours ago. It was encrypted but IT found a way through," Max continued.

"What was in it?" Adam asked. Catherine could swear she heard excitement in his voice.

"It was data about some airship being built in Iran. Information we already had for weeks now," Max said.

"Did they check well?" There might be some hidden folder. Megan liked to hide things in plain sight," Adam said.

"Drew worked on it," Max said. And to Catherine, "He's one of our best. He found nothing that would raise heads to her killer. There was a phone, and we are still going through the call logs to see who she may have spoken to, but all of it is nothing we don't already know. So we are back to square one."

Adam angrily kicked a chair as he groaned in frustration. Catherine pitied him and what he was going through. It must hurt as hell being unable to find the woman he loved killer, when he had the power to do so.

Catherine frowned as she recalled something that had happened months ago. At the time, she hadn't made much of it, but with all that was going on, she couldn't help but ponder over it.

"What's wrong?" Max asked, sensing a change.

"A couple of months ago, I received a call from an unknown number. I didn't know who it was. I heard screams and noises in the background. I was worried, and didn't know what was going on."

"Umm… That was Megan," Adam said with a grimace.

"What?" Catherine lifted a brow.

"A couple of months back, we had a fight. We... said pretty crazy things to each other, and she had to get back into her undercover duties with a mob group. She was drunk, and butt-dialed you. When she realized what was done, she decided not to bring it up, and hoped that you would forget it," Adam explained.

Catherine was disappointed that it wasn't a lead to follow up on. But at least she had gotten an explanation for that weird occurrence.

"I will let you know if something comes up," Max said softly.

Adam nodded at Max, and then at Catherine in a somewhat thank you as he headed out. Catherine hoped that they would be able to find closure so they could try to move on, no matter how difficult it was.

"I am sorry I let him in," Catherine said when they were alone. He gave her a look, and she knew he was pissed with her. "It's just that... he sounded really broken and I... I just... I couldn't leave him out there that way."

"You could have been hurt Cathie. What if it wasn't Adam? What if it was the killer who was lying to get in? Imagine if you had opened the door and he had stabbed you? Or knocked you out and taken you away? Did you think of all that? Did you even think of me before you made that decision?"

"I am sorry," Catherine said quietly. However, her apologies didn't seem to do much. He turned around and walked down the hallway, slamming his room door close.

She sighed. Yeah, he was right. Her encounter with Adam could have gone another direction. Would she have been able to escape whoever it was? She shuddered to even think of the outcome. To imagine herself trapped in the basement of an abandoned building out in the woods, where no one could hear her scream.

She knocked on Max's door, and for a minute or two, she thought he was not going to open up.

"What do you want?" he growled.

"Really, I am sorry Max. I shouldn't have, and I acknowledge that," Catherine said.

"I would never be able to forgive myself if something happened to you. After what happened with Megan, and with you earlier today, I am worried about you. I am not going to be there always with you. So I want you to be safe for me, for you, and for Megan. Please Catherine?" Max said.

"I will," she said, but she knew that if the opportunity to get hold of Megan's murderer came, she would jump at this, even if her life was in danger. "Forgiven me now?" she asked, with a smile.

"I don't know yet," Max shrugged.

She pressed her body to his, her smile growing wider as she felt his dick stir.

"Forgiven me?" she asked sleepily.

He chuckled as he said, "Of course yes!"

A MAN WATCHED in the shadows, waiting for her to return home. He waited for hours, until it turned dark, and his rage grew stronger. Where the hell was she? It took him another hour or so to realize that she was not coming home today.

As he headed back to the city, he tried to rein his anger. The bitch was getting on his nerve! He had tried to kill her out there on the road, and she had gotten away. There were limited opportunities to getting through to her and after this attempt, he was pretty sure the man she was fucking would take extreme measures to protect her. Yeah, she was probably with Max in his apartment or at a safehouse. His apartment he decided; the asshole would need her close to him.

He shrugged out of his jacket when he returned home. He headed for the decanter which still had some whiskey left and poured a glassful.

Time was running out. Every second that went by without him getting what Megan had left behind was critical. He could not afford for the truth to get out there. Not only would that destroy the organization's plans, he would be dead. No matter how valuable he was as an asset, he was dispensable.

He had been promoted before the debacle with Megan. The last thing he wanted was to be decommissioned. Everyone knew what that was. A suicide. Car accident. Gas leak. He had been involved in the decommissioning of other agents, and knew better than to fail the organization.

That night, he paid another visit to Megan's apartment, picking the lock on his way in. He knew he was grasping at straws by coming here, but he was getting desperate. Where had the bitch hidden it? She was not stupid to have hidden it here right? But then, she had probably kept it in plain sight.

He checked through her apartment, taking his time. He found nothing relating to her work. Well except for a bag up a vent in the kitchen that contained some guns, which he returned. Frustrated, he sat in the living room with a pissed look.

That bitch! He fucking wished he hadn't killed her. Should have kept her for weeks tied up, and interrogating her daily until she finally talked. Even her wouldn't be able to last that long without giving in. Now, he had no idea where she had kept the drive she mentioned.

The following day, he went to Max's apartment. It had taken him a couple of calls and money being exchanged for him to get his address. He grimaced as he walked across the street of the building. There were cameras outside the building, and right across. But that didn't stop him.

Ten minutes later, he returned with a delivery company T-shirt and cap, carrying an empty brown carton. He got into the building and then…

"How can I help you please?" a bald-headed security detail asked.

He sized him up, and then the other one who sat behind the desk. His eyes caught the rotating cameras in the lobby.

"I am here for a delivery," he said.

"Please drop the package and we will send it right up. Or inform the receiver to call us, so we can send you up," the security detail said.

He growled inside, however he flashed a smile at the detail. "Let me head out and make the call," he said.

He remained out the building for three hours, looking out for Catherine or Max, but he saw none of them. Getting in there was going to be pretty difficult, and unfortunately, not worth it. This pissed him even more. He recalled Megan's last words. "You not going to get it. I have made it so damn difficult for you," she had said with a coy and confident smile that taunted him in his sleep.

"I am going to find it," he said stubbornly. She had underestimated him, and he was going to make sure that all she had set out to protect was destroyed. Too bad, she would not be alive to see him victorious.

There was a possibility that Megan had been bluffing, but he doubted it. Megan had been damn serious. He was sure of it. If it was not at her apartment, at her lawyer's, then there was only one answer. It was with Catherine as he earlier suspected. Those two had been thick as thieves. Certainly, she would leave it to no other than Catherine. He doubted Catherine knew where it was, at least not right now. But like Megan, she was nosy, and she understood Megan pretty much

He would be watching Catherine closely. Very closely, from a distance. It was just a matter of time before she led him to the answers. And then, he would it take, and be unstoppable. Nothing was going to stand in his way.

CHAPTER 17

CATHERINE HAD SEEN those crime boards in movies, and they had always seemed quite appealing. However, it seemed so strange seeing her friend on a board, Max had worked on when he got up that morning. She moved closer, sipping her cup of coffee as she stared at Megan's picture at the top of it all.

Max had outlined her movements for the past two weeks leading up to her death. She had been in Mexico, days before she had come to France, working on a project Max didn't say much about, because his superiors hadn't told him either.

"There's so little they can tell me. We didn't work together, and it is best we know little about each other's jobs, unless they overlap," he told her.

"So what do we actually know? You guys have said that she had a lot of enemies. Who exactly? Were any threats made to her?" Catherine asked.

"The Iranians were pissed with her. She was on a case early this year where she revealed a war plan of theirs that set them back billions of dollars, sanctions and soldiers. Then, we have the Russians. We make enemies in our line of work," Max said. "She has received a couple of threats over the past years. Most of them were sent to the Bureau, because her identity has been kept secret. I was able to get a couple of these letters earlier," he said, referring to when he had gone out for a morning run.

He dropped a stash of letters on the table. Just as she reached for it, he touched her hand. "You are not going to like them," he warned.

"I am a big girl," she shrugged.

Max hadn't warned her firmly, she realized when she was done with the first letter. It was unsigned, but from the content and language, it had been written by a Middle Easterner, who had called Megan a slut who deserved to be decapitated. He had called her the devil's whore, and how he couldn't wait to dance with her head amongst his people. The hate in the letter made a shudder run through her. How could someone hate

Megan so much? She knew her friend had to have done crazy things to be respected as an agent, but to be hated so much by the other side?

The next letter was worse. The South Sudanese gang had threatened Megan's offspring to the sixth generation, stating that it would be his family's life-long goal to hunt them down and make sure they burned to ashes.

"I can't..." she shoved the letter aside. She couldn't deal with reading such terrible words about Megan. She would rather continue to hold onto her in positive light. "Did... I can't imagine Megan doing horrible things..."

"Whatever Megan did was sanctioned. And she did it for the good of this country," Max tried to reassure her.

"She killed?"

He nodded. "She did what was necessary."

It was hard to reconcile the Megan she knew to a murderer. She had always had a cold side to her, but to the extent of taking another life? She knew nothing.

"What about you?" she asked.

"I deal with negotiation. Done so since I got into the Bureau. However, have I killed in my line of work? Yes, twice. Once when I was in Tokyo and a negotiation deal went bad, and I was caught in a cross-fire. I had to get out of there or I was going to be killed," Max said.

"And the second time?" Catherine asked.

Max clenched his fist. "I was in Mexico for a negotiation deal with a drug lord. Hated his guts since I got the intel on him. He was a fucking asshole, who we was going to get into a deal with us, for some time off. Went over to his place in Mexico per his demands."

"You don't have to tell me," Catherine said, sensing how difficult the conversation was for him.

"He had a haram made up of underaged kids he had trafficked. Some of them he had killed when they tried to escape. It was sick… I couldn't deal with what he had done. To see those kids, locked up there, being abused by him and his men… I just couldn't let it go. So, I turned against him. My men were glad I gave the order, because they were pissed as hell. The mission was botched, but we got the kids out of there, and I got suspended for three months."

Damn! She hadn't expected that. "But you saved those children," she pointed out.

"The asshole was being watched for two years. It was a lot of time and resources. But if I was given the opportunity to do it again, I sure as hell would," Max smiled.

She was glad he had done what he needed to do. It made her realize how much of a bubble she lived in.

Despite how well-travelled she was, she had no idea the evil that was out there.

"We are following through with the letters, but a couple of the owners have been killed or gone into hiding since they were written. For most of them, this is not their first letter to the Bureau, directed to her agents. But I don't think the person who killed her wrote any of these letters," Max said.

"Who do you think killed her?" Catherine asked.

"I don't know," Max sighed. "But I think it was someone she knew, and worked with in the past. Maybe her cover got blown. Maybe she was involved in activities the Bureau was not aware of. This person knew where she was, and also knew our itinerary. This is no stranger. I want you to draw up a list of people Megan may have had a clash with over the past six months. Someone who could go this far to hurt her," Max said.

It was an easy job to do. There was only one person who Megan had a clash with in the past six months. Her building supervisor, Trey. At least the former one.

"Two to three months ago, she found him snooping around in her neighbor's apartment when she wasn't around. Don't ask me, I don't know how she knew, but she reported him to security, and he denied it. She threatened she was going to call the cops, and he attacked her, gave her a black eye."

Catherine had been so pissed, and had stated she was going to call the cops when Megan told her to be calm, that it had been handled.

"Hmmm…"

"What is it?" she asked.

"I heard something in the grapevine some while ago about Adam being almost suspended for beating a civilian up. I have a good idea who it is," Max said. One call to Adam, and he grudgingly confirmed it.

"He could have hurt her in retaliation, but how could he have gotten all the way to France? Why not do it here in the States?" Catherine pointed. "What?" she asked Max as he stared at her with a smile.

"You would make a pretty good agent," Max teased.

She rolled her eyes and he chuckled.

"You are right though. Doubt it is him, but that doesn't mean I would do a check on him, to see where he was a couple of weeks ago," Max said.

"Anything on Megan's lawyer?" Catherine asked. She had told him about the break-in, and was pretty sure it was connected to her friend's death.

"Unfortunately, the security in the building is terrible, so whoever got in didn't have any difficulty. We couldn't find any trace of the person. Also… approval has been given for her body to be released to you," Max said, looking at her with concern.

She blinked back tears. What came next after this? The cremation? Farewell? "I want to see her one last time," she said quietly.

Max shook his head. "You don't have to do this Cathie… She's not in a pretty good state, after all that has happened."

"Please, I need to see her. To look at her one last time," Catherine said. "Don't worry, I am a big girl," she added with a weak smile.

"I will make the call," Max said, after a moment.

She tried to focus on the board, but all she could think of was the picture of a dead Megan.

"I am going to find the asshole that killed you," Catherine swore to herself. It didn't matter how many years it would take, or how much it would involve, she was going to do right by her friend, and find her murderer.

The morgue had a solemn atmosphere. Catherine had no idea what death smelled like, but she was pretty sure it was that dark, depressing smell that lingered in the air, surrounded by dark shadows. She held on tight to Max's hand, and he squeezed back comfortably. Perhaps she should have listened to him instead, she berated herself. But she was here now, and she wasn't known for giving up.

They stopped in front of a metal door, and Max knocked on it. An older woman with grey hair, wearing scrubs opened it. Max introduced her as Maria, and she was in charge of the morgue. Her eyes widened and she gasped as she stared at a metal table.

"Oh God!" her hand flew to her mouth as she hurried to Megan, who was covered from a sheet from her chest down. Her skin was pale, with patches of darkness.

"We tried to clean her up as much as we could," Maria offered kindly.

She looked… peaceful. Her dear friend. Too peaceful. Her hand shook as she touched her best friend. Her skin was cold and tight. "I miss you Megan. Every single day. Every…" she whispered. It hurt seeing her friend like this. It was a final proof that this was no joke or elaborate scheme being pulled off by some sick reality show. No, this was real as hell. Her friend was dead, and gone for good. She was not religious, but a part of her hoped that there was a heaven and that someday she and Megan would reunite, and never have to deal with death and the sadness that followed.

"I love you Megan," Catherine said, giving her one last kiss on her forehead. Then she pulled away, bursting into tears as she fell into Max's arms.

"I am here, I am here for you," he whispered comfortingly, offering her support, as he led her away. She spared one last look at Megan, and promised herself that no matter how long it look, she would find the asshole or assholes, if they were a group, and have them pay.

She remained in the car while Max did the paperwork for the cremation, while looping Megan' lawyer in, so he could cover the cost.

"Three days. They want us back in three days to get her ashes," Max said when he returned.

She looked far into the distance. How could life be so abrupt? One minute you were happy and vacationing with your best friend, and the next you were saying goodbye to her at a morgue.

The ride back home was quiet. Even the car radios were turned off. Max understood that she needed to be left alone and said nothing. However, his presence was a great comfort to her. Just seeing and being around him, made her know that she was not alone.

She headed into the room and curled up in her bed when they got home. However, she could barely sleep. There was a lot on her mind, yet there was nothing to focus on. There was a knock on the door. She looked up and saw Max with lunch.

"I ordered takeouts," he said, placing a Chinese next to her.

"Thanks," she said, realizing she was pretty hungry. "I don't know what I am going to do moving on," she admitted. She doubted she could go back to living life like a normal person.

"I know you don't want to hear this right now, but there are a couple of jobs lined up for you since we returned," Max said.

Which she had always wanted. But right now, she doubted she had the stamina to pull them off. She was not going to be okay if she sat in front of cameras acting like everything was alright when it wasn't.

"I don't know Max, I think I might take a break from work," Catherine said.

"Are you sure about this?" Max asked.

"Are you asking as a manger or a lover?" she responded.

"As both actually. Taking a break right now may not be good for your career in the long run, as these companies will work with someone else, and the opportunities may not arise again. But at the same time, you need time to grieve," Max said.

He was damn right. She already had few offers, ad if she turned them down, those companies would work with someone else, and will most likely not reach out to her again in the future. "We can go over them later. See which one works for me right now. Maybe I need to distract myself with work to get over this," she added.

He put his arm around, and she cuddled into him. She was glad he was in her life during this tough time, as a lover and a friend. How on earth would she have been able to cope, if he wasn't in her life?

Catherine received her friend's ashes three days later in a black ceramic urn with intricate blue design. A whole human being with memories, reduced to speckles of ash, she thought sadly. It was what life was sadly.

She placed it on Max's mantle, staring at it. "I am going to be driving up to the lakes," she said to Max.

"We can do that later when all of this has settled down," Max said, offering her a glass of whiskey.

She shook her head. She wanted to get this over with, scatter the ashes in the lake, and make an attempt to move on with life. "I don't know how long things are going to take to settle. I want to do this…"

"Cathie…"

"Max, you don't have to come with me. I know you are busy and all." The past couple of days she had barely seen him. He had mentioned there some of their undercover agents had been exposed in some country in Europe, and they were working hard to mitigate losses. He was supposed to have flown out of the country, but had insisted that he's around to watch over her. "But I can go on my own and sort this out," she continued.

"I don't want you out of my sight," Max said stubbornly.

Catherine sighed. "You do realize I am not a kid right? I agreed to stay here a couple of days, and now you don't want me to leave?"

"I know you are not a kid, but we are dealing with a freaking murderer, Cathie. You don't have to be stubborn all the time," Max argued.

She glared at him. How dare he call her stubborn in such a manner? Like she was a three-year-old or spoiled brat. "It's also time for me to return home," Catherine said, hands on her waist.

"Come on Cathie! Let's not start again with this," Max growled.

"Yes we will, I can't hide in here forever. I have a life Max. I won't let anyone make me hide or live in fear. Never!"

"All I am saying is give a little more time before you head back to work, or leave town," Max said.

"Fine, but just for a few more days. I am going crazy being inside all day long like I am a wanted criminal," Catherine groaned. As much as she loved her privacy, being indoors all day was terrifying.

"Are you saying I have being a bad host?" Max teased.

She chuckled. He had been an amazing host. But she needed her own space to come to terms with all that had happened.

"Fine, I will stay. As long as you promise to continue being a good host," she smiled as she kissed him. They passionately kissed for what felt like an eternity. His hands slowly caressed her body, she gently rubbed her hand on his back. His kisses were soft, gentle, deep, and magical, their lips merged perfectly together.

Breathlessly, in the aftermath of the amazing sex, they laid together, talking quietly in hushed tones, as if there was an imaginary audience, they didn't want to hear them.

"Did you ever think it would be this good between us?" Catherine asked, running her fingers through his hair.

"Mmhm, I did," he said with a crooked smile.

Catherine chuckled. To be honest, she hadn't thought much of them in this position, and she had not been prepared for how amazing sex was between them. She wasn't bluffing when she said it was the best love she had ever had. Max was an amazing lover; he was tender and loving, concerned about her feelings even during the throes of passion. His affection was nothing she had encountered before. If she had known it was going to be this okay, just perhaps she would have made a move earlier she thought with an amused smile.

"What are you thinking of?"

Catherine woke up to an empty bed the following morning. She rolled over on the bed with a smile, thinking of how amazing last night had been. She could actually get used to it. For a moment, she felt guilty for being happy while her friend was dead. But she assured herself that Megan would have wanted her to be happy. Heck, she had been the one who suggested that Max was into her, and of course Catherine had been too blind to see it.

A note caught her eye. It was on the bedside table. Her smile disappeared when she read the content. "Hi Cathie. You were sleeping so peacefully and I didn't want to wake up. I am sorry, but I have to go away for a couple of days. It is really important, and I wish I didn't have to leave. But the orders come from high up. I want you to stay at the apartment while I am gone. I won't be accessible for a while, but once I am settled, I will call you."

"What the hell?" she glared. He expected her to just stay in his apartment while he was gone for God knew how long? She had her office. Her home. Her life!

Catherine fumed for most of the morning. She could not believe that after last night when she had told him that she wanted to go home, he had not only left her in his place, but also wanted her to be around. What was she supposed to do here, huh? Sit in front of the TV, watching old movies? Or continue ordering take outs? Social media was so annoying with videos and pictures of everyone outside, moving on with their lives.

The moment he called, she answered, "I am going home Max!" she told him. "You can't just leave me here, and expect me to wait for you. I have a life!"

"I am sorry I had to leave, but it is urgent. I knew if I woke you up, we were going to have a fight. I am just trying to protect you!"

"I didn't ask you to," she said quietly. He went quiet, and she wondered for a moment, if she had pushed too hard. But then she scolded herself. She had every right to be mad.

"You don't have to ask me to do the right thing Cathie. It is what Megan would have wanted, it is—"

"Well Megan isn't here anymore, is she? It is one thing having me cooped in here, but to travel and leave me here? I am going back home Max," Catherine said stubbornly. She knew she wasn't being fair to him, but she was overwhelmed with all that was going on at the same time, coupled with the frustration that Megan's murderer was still out there.

"Cathie, come on, stop acting—"

"Like a child. Yeah, you have said that before. And at this point, I really don't mind acting like one. Enjoy your trip Max, I am going home," she said, ending the call. She began to pack her personal effects into her bag. How dare he want her to stay here, hiding like a criminal, while he was away. Yes, there was a crazy murderer on the loose, but she was a full-grown human being!

The phone rang, with him calling back, but she ignored it. She knew what he was going to do, try to talk her to stay until he returned, but she had made up her mind. It was time for her to go home.

A couple of minutes later, Cathie headed back home in a cab. Her bags were in the trunk, and she held on to Megan's urn.

Devi barked excitedly, jumping at her as she got out of the cab. "I have missed you so much," Catherine said as she hugged her dog. It had just been a few days, but she had missed her little dog. Now she was back home and couldn't wait to feed her a lot of treats.

"Welcome home Catherine," Tehila smiled.

As she walked into her home, she knew she had made the right decision returning. There was no place better than home.

"Max called a couple of minutes ago. Said to inform him when you got here. Are you two fighting?" Tehila asked concerned.

"No, I don't think we are. Just giving ourselves a little space," she said. Hopefully when he got back, she would have gotten some more clarity about herself and all that was going on right now in her life.

She curled up in her bed, next to Devi, who didn't want to leave her side. It did feel good to be home, but she realized she kind of missed Max. Too early she told herself. She needed this, she assured herself.

The rest of the day went by fast. She went through her closet sorting out outfits she was going to give off to charity. It was pretty a tasking chore, and she wished she hadn't started it, and had gotten assistance instead. But once it began, she was on a roll.

Her phone rang as she was about getting into bed. It was Max. She wasn't in the mood to talk to him, and sent him a message that said, "I am okay".

The following morning, Catherine went over to her office. Natalie and Henry wrapped her in a group hug that had her chuckling.

"Guys, I am fine," she said, pulling away from them.

"You don't look it. You look like you barely slept last night," Henry said.

She grimaced as she stared at her reflection in the mirror. He was right. There were bags under her eyes. Last night, she had been uncomfortable in her bed, and it had nothing to do with the mattress. A part of her had been scared, and worried that she was not safe. A couple of times, she had jolted out of bed, with Max's name in her lips, only to realize that he wasn't around. But she was not going to admit that to him.

"I think you need to go on a vacation," Henry said.

She glared at him. No more vacations, at least anytime soon. The last one hadn't ended well. "Get me up to date on what has been going on," she said. Despite her not being around, she had gotten daily updates from them, but the past couple of days she had derailed. There was a new shipment of perfumes coming in next week. A reporter wanted to do an interview with her for a spread on a magazine about female entrepreneurs. There had been calls from Sonia, a renowned model who wanted to work on a limited perfume edition with Catherine.

"Sonia is annoying," Henry drawled. "Everyone who has worked with her hates her. I don't think you will be able to stand her pretentious ass."

"I will have a meeting with her, and that should determine if I get to work with her," Catherine said, knowing that people might be wrong about Sonia. But at the same time, they could actually be right, because it wasn't just from Henry she had heard such. Sonia was a young model, in her mid-twenties, and had a great fanbase both online and offline. It would be great to work with her, if she wasn't a headache. But she would have to let Max know. Thinking of Max, she wondered how he was doing. He hadn't told her where he had gone to, and she didn't bother to ask. Was this how his life was? Going and coming wherever the job demanded? What if he was in danger? Or if something happened to him and it was swept under the rug, just like in Megan's case? She didn't want to go through such an ordeal ever again.

"It is beautiful," Tehila said, referring to the urn that sat on the fireplace mantle. Catherine followed her gaze. She had brought it with her when she came down for breakfast. She knew she was being sentimental but she wanted Megan to be at the center of the home, watching over her. It gave her some sort of comfort.

"I still can't believe she's gone. Megan was so full of life. Intelligent. If I had known that was the last time I was going to see her, I would have made her favorite cherry cake for her," Tehila said.

"But you did make it for her," Catherine pointed out. The last time Megan had been here, Tehila had gone all out and Catherine had even feigned jealousy. "Remember?"

"Oh no, she came around when you were in France," Tehila said as she added spices into a pot of boiling broth.

It took a moment for Catherine to register what Tehila had just said. "Megan was here when I was in France?" she asked loudly.

"I thought you knew," Tehila frowned.

"When? What happened?" Catherine asked excitedly. This was news to her. Megan had not told her. Of course she would have.

"It was the… day you left. She came around in the afternoon, and I let her in. She went to your room, but she didn't stay for long, said she needed to get some things for you," Tehila said.

"I…" Megan had always been welcome to her home. But she had not told her to bring anything over for her. Besides, she was supposed to have been in Mexico at the time. Why had she come to the house? I will be right back," Catherine said, running off to her room.

She ripped open her closet, scouring shelf by shelf, as she tossed her clothes and shoes aside. She had no idea what she was looking for, but she had a strong feeling that Megan had left something here when she dropped by. It was the very thing her murderer was looking for.

For over an hour, Catherine went through every inch and corner of her room. She did find a couple of items she had forgotten about, like the blue ring she had gotten in Greece, and the pair of black heels she had thought she had given away, and Megan's cashmere sweater she had taken from her over four years ago. But she couldn't find what Megan had kept, and she would know whatever it was, because she looked around carefully.

Frustrated, she returned downstairs to Tehila. "Tehila, please," she took a deep breath. "I want you to think carefully. Do you know where she went to in my room? What Megan did? Asides my room, did she go somewhere else? Maybe the living room? Or here in the kitchen." The house was big, but she would devote a day to each room, and she was pretty sure that if Megan had left something for her, she would find it.

Tehila frowned at the question.

"You are not in trouble," Catherine assured her.

"I don't know… wait, I remember going out to the pool, and I saw her by the balcony. I waved to her, but didn't see me or respond."

"I will be right back," Catherine said, hurrying back to her room.

The doors opened into the balcony. Her eyes hovered around the almost bare space. Megan had always told her to do something with the space, like throw around a chair or something, but Catherine had wanted it empty, well save the flower pots on opposite sides. They were the one items out there. Perhaps Megan had just come around, she told herself, because there was nothing here. But it just didn't make…

Her eyes narrowed on one of the flower pots. Was it her imagination or the sand looked like it had been dug up. She hurried over to it and began to dig, the dirt getting into her finger. She sighed, realizing it was a dead end, when… she felt something. Her excitement bubbled as she latched onto it, pulling it out from the dirt.

It was a pair of keys. To a house, she supposed she thought as she stared at the bunch. On the keychain was written 10B, Winscourt. Her eyes widened in understanding as she connected the dots. She had been disturbed about something Megan had said in her letter, about having amazing fun at the apartment they had stayed in Winscourt. But down at the lake, they had stayed in a cabin by the beach. It had not been up to their taste, but they decided to make do with it. However, during their stay, while driving into town, they had seen a sign for an open house and had gone in. Well, Megan had dragged her in. The houses had been pretty, a bit small, but Megan had loved it. However, she had mentioned nothing about Winscourt since then.

Everything added up. In that little town, Megan had been so happy, and it was why she wanted her ashes spread out there. It was probably why she had decided to get another home there. She shoved the key into her pocket and grabbed her phone and bag, sending a quick message to Max.

"I am going to the lake. Winscourt! Megan had a house there!" she wrote. She was too impatient for him to return. Who knew how long it would take? Weeks? Or even months? Whatever was in Winscourt could not wait.

"I will be back soon Tehila, I need to lay Megan to rest," Catherine said as she took the urn from the mantle.

Her excitement brimmed as she got into the car. She had a feeling that whatever was at Winscourt would lead her to Megan's murder. There was no hiding anymore. The bastard was going to pay.

The Denton lakes was about a forty minutes-drive from the city. It was a quiet and exciting one for Catherine. There was so much on her mind. What if she was overreacting, and reading things wrongly? But how could she explain the set of keys? She pushed aside her doubts, and clung onto reality. Megan had left behind a message for her, and she was going to find it.

At the outskirts of Denton, she pulled up at a gas station to fill up her tank. Out here, the signal was pretty shitty. She sent a message to Max. *Headed out to Denton Lakes. I think Megan bought a house at 10B Winscourt.* I am sure there will be answers there. He would be pissed that she went there alone, but she couldn't wait for him, especially when she had no idea how long he was going to be away.

A car drove past her and for a moment, it looked familiar. She shook her head, dismissing the thought as she got into her car.

Her first stop was a small lake. The very lake she had camped out here months ago with Megan. The lake Megan wanted her ashes scattered in. It was quiet as she pulled into a deserted park. It wasn't tourist season, giving her the privacy, she yearned for.

She held the urn tenderly as she made her way through a clear-cut path in the woods. It was so calm and peaceful out here she thought. As the water came into view, she blinked back tears as she imagined Megan in the very spot close to the rock. Her friend laughing as she took pictures of Catherine making ridiculous poses. They had taken a selfie together; it was a happy picture of Megan she was going to have framed.

She found a place by the lake, close to a cave-like opening. There she sat, holding onto the urn. She didn't want to let go, if she was going to be honest. There was no bringing back her friend, and saying goodbye was difficult.

"I love you Megan. And I wish you were here with me, every blessed day," Catherine said. She reflected back to how they had met years ago, their journey of friendship and sisterhood, the ups and downs they had gone through together. She would never find a friend like Megan, and she was grateful for the memories and what they shared. She would never forget it.

Her hands shook as she opened the urn. And then she let it go, spreading her friend's ashes. As the wind dispersed the ashes, she could swear she heard her friend chuckling in her ear, telling her that everything was going to be just fine.

The car park was still empty when Catherine returned, her eyes puffy from crying. She had heard a car pull up when she was headed to the lake, she faintly recalled as she got into the car. She reached for her purse and pulled out her napkin, dabbing her eyes. And then... she heard it. A faint breath, making her realize she was not alone in her car. Her eyes widened in recognition as she glanced for a moment at the person in the backseat.

She reached for her door handle, but it was too late. A cloth went over her nose, overwhelming her with a heavy chemical smell that instantly made her eyes drop close.

CHAPTER 18

CATHERINE FELT LIKE shit. Like her head had been smacked on a wall, with the resounding pain she felt in her head. And her mouth tasted really dry, like she was stranded in a desert for days without water.

"Water…" she whispered as she swallowed her spit, her hand struggling to reach for… Her eyes sprung open, as she fought hard against the ropes that bound them. Her memory was hazy for a moment, but it all came back to her. The person in the car!

"Welcome back."

She glared at him. "Dave, what the hell do you think you are doing?" she snapped. "Get me out of these ropes right now!" Her voice shook as he took steps closer to her. There was something off about him that terrified her. His small presence loomed over her menacingly, and his eyes, they were wild and filled with anger and hate. She had never seen him like this and it terrified her.

"You can shout all you want, no one is going to hear you," Dave said.

She looked around quickly. She was in a wooden shack, with boxes stored up. She had no idea where she was. Was she even in Denton anymore?

"What do you want Dave? Is this about the money Megan gave to me? I told you I was going to give you some of it," Catherine said. She guessed if she was in his position, she would feel bad as well, and so she had made the decision to give him some of the money.

Dave laughed. "I have to say, that was well-played by the cunt. Not even giving me a penny. But I am not going to take the scraps you give me. I want none of that shit!" he spat.

"Then what do you…" Her eyes widened, and for the first time ever, she understood what fear truly was as she looked up into those dark eyes that reeked of evil. She shook her head slowly, refusing for it to be true. "No, you didn't…" she whispered. There was no way that Dave had killed Megan. Definitely no way!

He knelt beside her, and she flinched as he caressed her face with his rough fingers. "Oh yes, I did. I killed her. Five knives. Nine stabs. That was what it took to kill her," he sneered.

"No, no, you are lying," Catherine said as tears welled in her eyes. All of this had to be a sick twisted joke, because it just didn't make sense.

"Hi Catherine. Let's meet in five minutes at Le Blu Café in town for a brief meeting about the shoot. Ernesto," Dave said sweetly.

Of course, she remembered the message! It had been in the note. The one delivered to her room at the resort. The very message that had made her leave the resort, and when she had returned, Megan had been missing.

"You sent the message! You killed her! You are shameless! Heartless!" she cried out as he struck her across the face.

"Shut the fuck up!" he yelled at her.

Catherine went quiet. Then quietly said, "Why? Why did you kill her? She loved you."

Dave chuckled. "Oh no, she fucking loved herself. And you too. Fucking loved her damned job and was going to sell me out! No matter how much I begged her. How I told her to just fucking let this one go, she just didn't!"

"What… what are you talking about?" Catherine asked confused.

He smiled cruelly, sending shivers all over her body. "I should kill you, and dump your body in the water. But you and I have a lot to do… so I am going to tell you a story. A story of how a nobody became a somebody."

He pulled out a pack of cigarette from his pocket and lit it up, taking a puff and blowing it in her face. She coughed, and he chuckled, clearly enjoying her discomfort.

"Megan is not the only smart one you know. But everyone thought she was the smart one. Oh, Megan got a scholarship to an Ivy League. Oh, Megan is at the top of her class. Megan, Megan, Megan. It was always all about her. But you know I went to an Ivy League right? I was at the top of my freaking class, just like Megan. And I was supposed to be offered an opportunity to work for the FBI just like Megan!"

"She told you?" Catherine whispered.

"I am not stupid like you pretty face. Everyone who was smart could see she was an agent. I was supposed to be an agent. I did everything right. Applied over and over again, and got turned down. I wrote letters. Met with sleazy directors at the pub, who didn't give a shit about my brains! Years upon years, and I was turned down of the opportunity to serve this country. Dejected and sad, I took a break, and left this shitty country," Dave said, taking a drag from the cigarette.

Catherine faintly recalled Megan mentioning that Dave had suddenly transferred and gone to Russia to continue with his studies.

"In Russia, I realized my potential. It didn't take long for me to be noticed," he snapped his finger. "They valued me for who I was. They saw me for who I truly am, an asset. The NABT recruited me and made me who I am today!"

Catherine was not much of a political person, but she definitely knew who the NABT was. It was a terrorist group which had been operating in Eastern Europe for over thirty years, with networks rumored to be spread across other continents. They were responsible for series of attacks including bombings, kidnappings and crimes against humanity. They were a thorn in the asses of several governments, especially the American government who had suffered from their terrorist acts.

"You betrayed your country," Catherine said.

Dave chuckled. "My country betrayed me when I was refused to serve. But the NABT have embraced me, and showed me what the future should be. My life was great. Awesome! Until Megan decided to stick her nose in my business. I don't know how she did it, but the fucking bitch found out!"

Catherine jumped on the seat as Dave kicked a bucket.

"She invited me over for lunch you know. Said we needed to talk, and I fucking thought she wanted to apologize for being a bitch all these years. You know what she did?" he grabbed her face, staring down at her.

Catherine shook her head. Of course, she didn't know.

"She showed me pictures, phone recordings, mail trails. That snake had been watching me for years and knew I was working with the NABT!" He sounded disappointed that Megan had found him out.

"She was going to expose you," Catherine said.

His cold eyes rested on her. "Not if I worked for her and gave her intel. She wanted me to betray the people who had embraced me so she could get another pretty trophy and a pat on the back. And so I told her to give me some time…"

"While you planned how to kill her," Catherine added quietly.

"Ooohh… I loved killing her. The thrill of it makes me feel in control. I watched her you know, right across the airport when she arrived. Watched you both while you were at the resort. I had the perfect plan, and it was almost ruined when that idiot came around," Dave spat.

Adam! He was referring to Adam.

"But it was just my fortune that they had a lover's spat and he was out in no time. She was too distraught to see me coming down that road. And when you left, all I have needed. All I have wanted was delivered to me. She fought against me. Struggled, but I knocked her out. And when she came to…" He smiled, caressing her face. "I destroyed her."

"You are a monster!" Catherine spat. She didn't care if he struck her again. He was a terrible person, and she wished that Megan had exposed him when the opportunity arose. "You can kill me, but I will let you know that you won't get away with this! You won't!"

"The rants of a poor fool who knows her time is up," Dave chuckled. "I am going to kill you, and I will enjoy every moment. But not yet. I still have need for you. You are going to help me find the information Megan had on me and other members of NABT. I checked through her fucking apartment but it wasn't there! The fucking lawyer's office. But you know where it is, don't you," Dave dangled the house key. "You knew her better than anyone. You are going to help me find that information, and who knows, I may give you a fast death."

Catherine screamed as he reached for her. Her scream was shortened as he shoved a cloth into her mouth. She fought feebly as he removed the ropes from the chair, tying them around her hands as he pushed her out the door.

He was right. No one would have heard her scream. There were in a cabin out in middle of nowhere, deep in the woods. Night had arrived, the sky completely dark, with stars twinkling in the distance. He pushed her through the woods. She stumbled a few times, and he grabbed her arm, pushing her hard.

At a clearing, his black truck was parked. Her eyes widened in recognition. Yes, she had seen his truck while she was headed to Denton. And then! She screamed into the cloth. He removed it from her mouth to hear what she had to say.

"You tried to kill me!" she said. Those boots which he wore now, she had known there was something about them. And the black truck that had run her over weeks ago, it was his! How could she have been so blind? Anger grew in her for being so stupid. By now, he should be behind bars.

"A stupid move on my part. I was upset you know after the will reading. I am never going to lose my guard again," Dave reassured, sounding disappointed with himself, as he shoved the cloth back into her mouth.

He opened his car trunk and gestured at her to get in. Catherine shook her head. Hell no! She gasped as he pointed a gun to her forehead.

"I am not going to repeat myself again. Get in," Dave warned.

She quickly got into the trunk, gasping in fear as it was shut in her face. A moment later, the car began to move. She tried to hit the roof of the car with her knees, yelling into the cloth in her mouth. But the car was on high speed and no one could hear her cry for help.

Tears welled in her eyes and she fought hard to prevent them from falling. Was this how she was going to die? Killed by Dave who would probably bury her in a shallow grave, or dump her body somewhere no one would find her? No one knew she was out here. Max was faraway and by the time he returned home, she would be long gone.

Oh poor Max. The man had shown her what happiness was in the past weeks. He had given her what she had yearned for, for several years. She was going to miss him, she thought with resignation as a tear slid down her face. She should have been kinder to him; listened to him because all he had wanted was her best interest.

She was even going to miss her terrible family, and the opportunity to tell him how horrible they were to their faces. And Devi! Her amazing and robust puppy. She was going to miss her work, her friends, her life... All of it! She didn't want to die, but she was being realistic that it was her fate. She wondered if this was Megan felt as well.

She wondered if anyone was looking for her. Certainly not Tehila. She had told her she was going to be spending the night over at Dentor. Max was probably busy, and had no idea where she was. She would be long dead by the time he returned home.

"Oh God! I don't want to die," she whispered in tears. There was so much she wanted to live for. To expand her business. To explore the possibility of reuniting with her horrible family. To tell Max about her feelings for him. But tonight could bring an end to all her dreams and hopes.

"It's going to be alright," she heard herself saying, trying to reassure herself. But how the hell was she supposed to get out of this situation? Her hands were tied, and her mouth sealed from crying out for help. She wished she had gone on one of those survival drills Megan had tried to enroll her for, but she had always too busy. Maybe then she would have known how to remove a knot, but with how mean Dave was, she doubted he would have tied the knot that easy for her to be free.

Suddenly, the car stopped. She strained to listen, but all she got was silence. And then… another voice.

"Good evening officer," she heard Dave say.

"Help! Get me out of here!" she began to scream into the cloth, making frantic kicks at the roof of the trunk with her knees.

"Let me have your ID," the officer said.

She continued making a sound, but it was a feeble attempt. He could not hear her. Tears slid down her eyes at the failed opportunity as the truck began to move again. She laid back, accepting her fate.

A couple of minutes later, at least she supposed so, the truck came to another stop. She heard footsteps, and then a grating sound, like a garage was being opened. He got back into the truck and drove for a second or so, before stopping.

"Shit!" she heard him call out. And then the trunk was opened.

Dave stared at her with glee, and she glared at him. She yelled mumbled curses at him as he dragged her out of the trunk.

Her eyes ran over her new environment. They were in the garage of a house. A new house from the look of things with the buckets of paints lined up against the wall, and the covered furniture on one side. She realized where this was; Megan's home in Winscourt.

"Move!" he said, pushing her towards a door. There was a security system set up, and she hoped that this would prevent them from getting in. She had barely prayed on this when Dave pulled out a little tab from a black bag, he had with him. He plugged it to the security system and there was a beep sound, as the door opened.

So, that was how the asshole had gained access into her home. There was no doubt now that he was the one who was responsible for the break-in at her home. All this while, he had been watching and planning. She had been a fool to trust and feel pity for him, but then, how could she have known any different?

They walked into a dark space. Dave left her for a moment while he looked around for a light switch. It came on, and a smile spread on her lips as they found themselves in the kitchen which was still under construction. It was gorgeous, with its marble tabletop, and stainless-steel double sink and taps. Megan had gone with a brown simple look, but damn did it look really good. The tiles were still being done, but she could imagine the finish look.

When they had come around for the open day, it had a décor from the nineties, with its ugly red décor, and wooden floor. Megan had really wanted to set up a home here, she realized, for her to devote so much time and attention here. It was just so freaking sad, she would never live to see this place become more.

"This would be a cool place to live," Dave said. He chuckled as she glared at him. If he dared to as much as live here, she would haunt him every blessed day, until he went crazy. Who knew, she might just link up with Megan in the afterlife, and they would make living so terrible for Dave, he would have no option than to off himself.

The living room was still very much under construction with the walls bare, the previous wallpapers had been removed; there were a couple of furniture which had been covered by drapes.

Dave shoved her to the ground, against a furniture.

"You stay here! I am going to look around. Who knows, I might not have need for you," he smiled cruelly. "Don't think you can try to escape, I got the keys," he added, dangling the bunch.

She looked around the dim room as he walked into a corridor, leaving the door open. The lights were off and the only source of light into the room was from the floodlights above. Grimacing in pain, she staggered up. Quietly she approached the window, staring out to get a glimpse of where she was. She could see a couple of houses around, but from what she could recall, most of these houses were unoccupied, and it was during the tourist season that they were occupied. It was most likely that they were alone or almost alone in the neighborhood.

The fireplace had been completed, with a picture Catherine recognized. It was one of her and Megan at the lake. It was a selfie she had insisted they take. Megan had framed it, she thought with a sad smile. That trip had meant more than she had thought to Megan, for her to make the big move of buying a home out here.

"Fuck!" she heard Dave yell down the hallway. She quickly went over to where she had been, anticipating his return.

"Where did she keep it?" he snapped at her.

"I don't know what you are talking about," Catherine said. Up until a couple of hours ago, she had no idea that he was part of a terrorist network.

"You are lying to me bitch! You were her fucking best friend! Of course you knew!" She cried out as he grabbed her arm, pulling her to his face. "You are going to tell me where she kept it! You fucking will!"

She cried out as he dragged her down a hallway, tossing her into a bedroom, that had only a bed and some trunks which Dave had ripped open, tossing out the items, which she figured had belonged to the former owner.

He kicked her, and she cried as he shoved her on the ground. "Start looking!" he instructed.

She lifted up her hands to him, resisting the urge to roll her eyes. Couldn't he see that her hands were tied? For a moment, he hesitated, but then he pulled her to him and began to unravel the knot.

"You try anything stupid and I will kill you," Dave said coldly. She knew he wasn't joking. He would out-rightly kill her.

She stretched her arms as he set her free. Then turned her attention to the trunks. She began to pick up the items, going through them, having no idea what exactly he actually wanted her to find.

"I have gone through all of that!" he snapped.

"Do you want me to help or not? What exactly am I looking for?" she asked. Was it a flash? Envelope? Video? She had no freaking idea.

"A flash most likely. An envelope perhaps. You will know when you see it. Anything you find, and I mean anything, show me. You are too dumb to know what may be useful," he added.

Catherine rolled her eyes. It was not surprising that he thought that of her. Not only was he a killer, he was a chauvinistic killer. How grand. And to think all this while, she had thought him to be shy and calm. Under that mask had been hiding a monster.

He was right. There was nothing there that was of help. He dragged her to the next room, which also had a couple of items stored from the previous owners. Together, they went through the items, but it was clear that whatever Megan had hidden wasn't here. Or perhaps it was so well hidden, they could not find it. And that meant, he would kill her soon, when he realized she was of no help. Any moment from now, she expected him behind her, his hand around her neck while he strangled her to death. Or perhaps, plunging a knife into her as he had done with Megan. Or he could use the gun he had threatened her with earlier. There were so many ways he could kill her, and it terrified her.

Was she really going down without a fight, she wondered? To let Dave kill Megan and herself just like that? It surely couldn't be that easy. She couldn't let him get away with it, and for the rest of his life, consider himself smarter and better than everyone else. She couldn't let him get away. She knew she was going down, but she was not going to make it easy for him.

"Found something!" Catherine called. As expected, he hurried to her side. Just as he got to her, she aimed her knee in between his thighs, hitting hard with every ounce of strength she could summon.

Dave groaned, falling to his feet. She hit him again quickly, and he cried out in pain. It was the opening she needed. She ran out of the room, hurrying to the front door. She removed the bolt, but it was bloody locked with a key. She began to scream, "Help me! Help me!! Somebody help me!" she cried, as she ran to the kitchen. Dave had locked the door leading to the garage, she realized as she tugged hard at the door.

"Where are you! You fucking bitch!" she heard him yell.

She was trapped in there, she realized, as her heart pumped with adrenaline. She looked around for any object, a knife, a bat, but the kitchen was fucking empty.

"There you are," Dave sneered, standing in the doorway. She ran to the door and began to pound on it, despite knowing that it was not going to budge. He lifted his gun, pointing it at her. "You fucking bitch! I am going to kill you!" he said.

She squealed as he dragged her hair, pulling her to the living room where he tossed her on the floor.

"You are fucking useless! I never gave Megan the opportunity to say her last prayer, but I am going to be kind this time around," Dave smiled as he pointed the gun to her temple.

"I… know where it is," Catherine said, as she looked ahead to the fireplace.

Dave chuckled. "Your little trick is not going to work on me this time around," he said.

"I am not lying! I know where it is!" she said firmly.

He must have sensed her honesty, because he pulled away, watching her through suspicious eyes. "Where is it?" he asked.

"I know you are going to kill me when you get it, but I am only going to tell you on one condition," Catherine said.

Dave laughed. "You are not in the position to make demands."

"Then kill me, you are going to do it either way, and you will still not find that drive. And every day, you will keep looking over your shoulder, knowing that the drive is out there spelling your doom," Catherine smiled.

"What do you want?" Dave asked.

"A phone call," Catherine said.

Dave laughed until tears rolled down his eyes. "You think I am stupid? I am not going to let you call for help, although it would be too late, since you would be dead. But I am not going to let you rat me out before I leave the country tonight."

"Then a text. You can see what I am going to send," Catherine said.

He thought over her request for a moment then nodded. "You get your text, but after you show me where the drive is," Dave said.

She wanted to tell him she would only show him where it was after the text had been sent, but she knew that was pushing too far.

"Fine, I am going to trust you Dave, and hold on to your word," Catherine said. She only hoped that he would be a gentleman, and live up to his promise. There was one person she wanted to send that final message to. Max. The one she cared the most about, and he deserved to know that she loved him.

"Enough with the games! Where the fuck is it?" Dave asked.

He pointed the gun at her as she staggered up. She went towards the fireplace mantle, where the picture frame sat. It had seemed odd to her when they first arrived, that despite the emptiness of the house, Megan had left a picture frame of the two of them. Her suspicion had grown when she was forced into a search in the bedrooms, which barely had any personal effects of Megan. Why would Megan leave a picture of them right here? She might be grasping at straws, but she had a feeling that the answer was in the frame.

It was one of those wooden frames that you had to dismantle to put a picture in, then slid a glass over it. Her hands shook, under Dave's menacing and curious gaze as he watched her dismantle the frame.

She gasped, her heart racing fast as she stared at it, a black flash drive in the back of the frame.

"What is it?" Dave said, sensing her change of mood.

He quickly grabbed the frame from her and his eyes lit up as he stared at the drive. "This is it, right?" he asked, but she knew he wasn't referring to her. "This is it!" he repeated, as if trying to assure himself that whatever was in the drive was the information he needed, the one Megan had on him.

"I gave you what you wanted, now you have to keep to your promise," Catherine said quietly.

His cold eyes turned to her, and she gulped. She had been a fool to hope that he would be a gentle-

man. He was an asshole who didn't care about anyone but himself.

"Are you really that naïve Catherine? Of course
not. Get on your fucking knees!" Dave snapped.

Tears welled in her eyes as she did as he com-
manded. This was how she was going to die, and it
hurt her badly. She had hoped that death would come
to her in old age, but perhaps this was better, a sudden
death, leaving behind those she cared about.

"Say hi to Megan for me," Dave said, as he raised
the gun to her.

Catherine closed her eyes, willing to embrace
death as it extended its arms towards her. Suddenly,
chaos descended. There was a loud scream, which she
would realize came from her as the door was kicked off
its hinges. At the same time, a gun went off. This was
it, she told herself as she squeezed open her eyes. And
then, just as she wondered what death felt like, she felt
familiar arms wrap around her.

Her eyes opened, widening as she stared right at
Max. "Max!" she cried as tears freely rolled down her
eyes. She hugged him tight, not willing to let go.

"I am here for you Cathie, I am here," Max reassured her.

It was then she realized they were not alone. She pulled away from him and gasped as she saw Dave dead on the floor, a bullet hole gaping in the middle of his head.

"I killed him," Max said with a proud smile.

The room was now filled with federal and local officers, who were scouring the scene, as Dave was being bagged.

"He has the drive," Catherine said, as one of the officers handed the bagged drive to an older man with grey hair.

"My boss," Max said.

"We need to have her checked," one of the paramedics said.

Catherine shook her head, not wanting to let go. It all seemed like a surprise to her, how he had found her, and how they had all gotten here just before she was killed.

"I will be with you very soon," Max said.

Reluctantly, she pulled away from him, following the paramedic who led her to an ambulance outside. Her vitals were checked, and she winced as the paramedic placed a plastic over the bruises she had gotten when he had smacked her.

"I am here," Max said, joining her in the ambulance. She hugged him, so freaking glad that he had come at the time he did. One second more, and she would be dead.

"How… how did you know?" she asked.

"I got your text, while I was in the airport tonight, still trying to sort my bags," Max said. "I tried calling you but your number was unreachable. I went to the Bureau, and I almost punched my boss, when he told me there was nothing that could be done. That you were none of the Bureau business, but I knew something was wrong. I just knew it! We called the local cops who found your vehicle abandoned at the lake with no signs of you. It was at that point my boss decided to call in the troops. You have no idea how worried I have been about you. I thought I was going to lose you."

"I thought I was going to die. That I would never see you again," Catherine said. She had been so close to death, barely inches away from it, she could swear she had seen the light, and heard Megan call out to her from the other side. It was a miracle she was alive.

He caressed her face, and their lips met in a kiss. Her arms wrapped around him as she tasted him. God, how much she had missed this man! They pulled apart at the clearing of someone's throat. It was Max's boss, who he introduced as Tim.

"How are you feeling?" he asked.

"Okay, I guess. I just need some rest, and maybe a couple of sessions with my therapist," she added with a giggle, but she wasn't joking. Today had been traumatic for her, and it would take some time for her to deal with all that happened, and move on.

"We would like to get a statement from you," Tim said.

"Tim, let's do this some other time," Max said, with a glare.

"The earlier we have this done, while her memory is fresh, the better," Tim insisted stubbornly.

Max wrapped his arm around protectively, holding his boss' gaze, as if daring him to ask her any question.

"Don't worry Max, I will do it and get it over with," Catherine said. She gave him a firm smile. it was best she relieved the terrible experience now that it was still young, so she could move on with her life.

"I am going to be present," Max said, and he was not asking for permission.

For the next twenty minutes, Catherine was faced with tons of questions by Tim and another officer. She held on tight to Max as she relived her ordeal with

Dave. As she repeated what had happened, it dawned on her how lucky she was to be alive. She had been right in front of a hardened murderer with a large ego, who enjoyed playing mind games. He would never had let her go, and if Max hadn't come at that time, she would have just been another body he had left behind in a trail of blood.

"We will reach out to you if we have further questions," Tim said.

She was more than glad to be out of their presence, relieved as she got into Max's car. She sighed, resting her head on the seat. "So, what happens now?" she asked.

"Further investigation will be done. The drive is still being accessed. If truly Megan left something behind that implicates Dave and NABT, then we can bring them down," Max said.

"And Dave?" she asked. He was dead, and she was damn glad. It had either been her or him.

"He was dead on arrival. I damn well would kill him again if I had to," he flashed a smile at her. "What is on the drive, and the investigation that follows will determine how much would be told to the public."

Catherine scoffed. She knew bloody well that nothing of such news would be revealed to the public, and she agreed with that. Such news would stir up the public, and may cause panic. Also, it would also alert members of the NABT group, that the US government was onto them. With the damage and deaths they had caused, she wanted them to go down by all means.

They pulled up in front of a hotel. It was a long way from home, and they needed to rest, especially Catherine who had had a pretty long day. It was a small cozy hotel, with an empty reception, manned by an older man. He took one look at them, and handed them a key.

"We don't want any disturbance," Max instructed him.

The room was small, occupied by a king-sized bed which Catherine craved for. She stepped out of her clothes, into the bathroom, wincing as warm water cascaded over her body, against the bruises. She sighed, her arms aching. It felt like she had gone hiking, her body was sore, and she had a feeling she would hurt pretty bad when she woke up in the morning.

"Hey."

She leaned onto him, as his arms wrapped around her from behind..

He wrapped a clean towel around her, patting her dry, and another towel over her hair.

The smell of coffee woke Catherine up the following morning. As expected, her body hurt. Max offered her a cup of coffee, and a plate of sandwich which had been brought by room service.

"Any news?" she asked.

"Yes, I spoke to Tim a few minutes ago. The flash drive checked out. What is on it is unbelievable. He was so freaking excited. There's enough to track down most of NABT members who have remained hidden across countries for years. Megan… the information she gathered is mind blowing. It is no wonder they killed her," Max said excitedly.

Catherine smiled. It was sad that her friend had died in the process of unraveling the truth, but because of her, millions of lives would be saved. "Thank you," Catherine whispered to Megan. She hoped she could hear her wherever she was, and see how grateful she was for everything she had done, not just for her, but also for her country.

"So what happens now?" Catherine asked.

"We go home, and try to move on from this," Max said.

"Thank you, Max," Catherine said. She would always be grateful to him for showing up when he did.

"You don't have to thank me for anything. I will do it over and over again, for the woman I love," Max said.

Her eyes widened at his words. She stared at him and he nodded. "Hell yeah, I fell for you the first day I saw you at that party. You walked in and I got blown away. You have no idea how much I have wanted to be with you, but I was worried that telling you my feelings would get in the way of our friendship. I was bloody scared Catherine. I thought I had lost you and I kept on berating myself for not being with you. For leaving. If something had happened to you, I don't know what I would do. I fucking love you Catherine," Max professed.

"And I love you too Max! I love you!" she cried excitedly. To hear him say those words to her made her heart leap in excitement.

A wide smile spread on his lips, and then he kissed her. The kiss deepened and with every touch she felt his love for her. She had no idea where their journey was going. But what she did know was that she loved this man and looked forward to spending forever with him.

"You down with spending another night here?" Max asked, as he pulled his shirt over his head.

She chuckled. Hell yes!

He was tender with her, holding her gently as he kissed her softly. So softly she wanted more of him, her arms wrapped around his neck, pulling him closer to her. She sighed as he pulled away from her. Her eyes opened and she stared up at him. His gaze on her was so intense she wanted to find some place to hide. He could see right through her. He could read her thoughts, her deep love for him that scared and excited her at the same time. And in those dark eyes of his, she read his promise of forever. She wanted him in that very moment to take all of her and express his undying love for her.

# EPILOGUE

CATHERINE SMILED AS she watched Devi fetch the Frisbee, she threw at her. She returned to her for a scratch. "You are doing good girl," Catherine said.

"How are my girls doing?"

Her smile grew wider as Max joined them by the garden. He had with him a bouquet of rose which Catherine took a long sniff of, basking in their scents. He knelt in front of her, placing his head on her bump. In that moment, she felt their daughter move. She was always so responsive to his presence. This one, was going to be a daddy's girl, and Catherine couldn't wait to spoil her rotten.

About a year ago, Catherine had gotten married to Max, in a little intimate wedding, attended by those she cared about. She had extended an invite to her family, but they had been too busy, which was disappointing since she had tried to be there for them after her near-death experience. But it was clear that they did not care for her, and she had decided not to push further to be in the lives of those who didn't want her.

As she walked down the aisle that morning, she had known that it was the right decision. All the years of waiting for that special someone was worth it, as Max was the one. In his touches, words and actions, he made it clear that he loved her, and would continue to protect her for the rest of their lives.

The past year had been amazing, as they had gotten to know each other more, and explore the union called marriage. They had gotten a smaller house in the neighborhood, with more acres for Devi to run wild. Every day, he reminded her of how much he loved her.

Their joy had increased immensely when she found out she was pregnant. It was unbelievable how so much had happened in the past month. Earlier in the day, she had stood in front of her mirror, staring at her heavy bump. It still seemed like a dream, but she was going to be a mother, and she could not be happier.

"How was work?" she asked, as Max settled next to her.

"Great. You will see it on the news, we cracked down on a NABT cell here in Florida," Max said.

She grimaced when he mentioned the terrorist group. For the past year, the FBI had intensified their actions in bringing them down. Megan's secret project was massive, revealing networks of cells, that would have taken the Bureau decades to gather. She had received a posthumous award for her bravery, which had been received by Catherine, who was damn proud of her best friend.

"And Adam?" she asked.

Adam had become an integral part of their family. Well, Max had resisted at first, as he bore mistrust towards the other man, but Catherine had seen way past that. If Megan could love and accept him, then he wasn't that terrible. And he had proved this over the past year. He was an amazing man, and had become a close friend of Max. If Max wasn't available, she could always count on him. Anytime, any day.

"He's in Egypt, he should be flying back in today. Said he got something for the kid," Max grimaced. For the past month, Adam returned with a gift for their child, and it was an absurd and gigantic gift like the life-size giraffe he had gotten from Kenyan. Max had stumbled upon it one night, and had almost fought with it, thinking it was an intruder. There was no doubt Adam was going to make a great uncle.

She was seeing a therapist, and was coping with her grief and loss, but the truth was, she really missed her friend. She had taken so much for granted, and was grateful for the moment spent with her. So many times, she found herself going over her pictures and the stolen videos she had made when they were together. Megan would always be a huge part of her life. Always. There was no bringing her back from the dead, but she would make the most of her memory. She had set up a foundation in her name to help girls in foster homes get into colleges to further their education. In about a year, they had helped three girls get into college, and she hoped to help more girls in the coming years. Megan didn't give a shit about such charity crap, but she knew she would love the idea, and giving girls the opportunity to have better lives.

Her business was thriving, in a better place than it had been in the past years. There were so many collaborations and purchases, that she had hired more hands, and was thinking of expanding. She could not be happier than she was.

"Are you okay?" Max asked as she squeezed his hand.

"Just a bit of pain," Catherine said. It certainly wasn't just her imagination but when she thought of Megan, her little girl kicked. Max said she could probably feel her change of emotions, but this time around it was different, as another bout of pain hit her.

Devi barked excitedly, dancing around Catherine as she stood up. "I think I am going to lie down and have some rest," Catherine said. "What?" she asked Max as he stared at her stunned.

She followed his gaze and her eyes widened as she stared at the floor beneath her. Her water had broken and her dress was stained. "Oh my God! Oh my God!" she panicked. It couldn't be happening now right? She wasn't due for about three more weeks.

"Cathie, it is going to be okay. Take a deep breath my love," Max said, taking her arms gently. "Tehila!" he called as they got into the house.

The older woman hurried over to them. "Please get the bag!" Max called to her, as the woman raced upstairs to get the bag Catherine had taken her time to prepare for the delivery.

The contractions intensified as they drove to the hospital. She placed a hand over her bump, and softly reassured her girl to remain calm. They were going to be in the hospital soon.

Max arrived at the hospital within the shortest time possible. She could sense him panicking about, and tried to remain calm. Two parents could not panic at the same time.

"I am with you my love," he said as she was wheeled into the hospital. He was not leaving her side. Never. He always reassured her.

Two hours later, Catherine cried out in relief as her child came into the world, a little cry filling the room. Tears filled her eyes as her baby girl was placed in her arms. She looked up to Max who had been with her all through, not for a moment losing control. They shared a smile as they said in unison, "Megan". They had decided they were going to name their little damsel Megan.

Megan smiled, a beautiful smile that in that moment said yes, she loved and accepted her name. Catherine could swear that she did look so much like her best friend.

"She loves the name," Catherine smiled.

"Who wouldn't?" Max said, putting an arm around her. She rested on his shoulder comfortingly and felt bliss that she could not explain. Here, she was at home, with the man she loved, and a beautiful daughter. She could not be happier.

Two years later. All seems to be quiet after their horrific adventure…but is it?

Catherine drives into town in her white Range Rover and notices that this dark colored Suburban SUV seems to be following her, she pulls up in the parking and heads for the bank.

Later when driving back the car is gone but before entering her driveway the car crosses her on the other side heading off into the distance, terrified she goes into the house and tells Max what just happened.

Max says (with a dark scary sound in his voice) …. This can't be happening. Don't worry, I will fix it once and for all.

Later that day Catherine gets a text message on her phone "I promised to protect you" "Call you later.

MORE AMAZING BOOKS FROM THIS AUTHOR

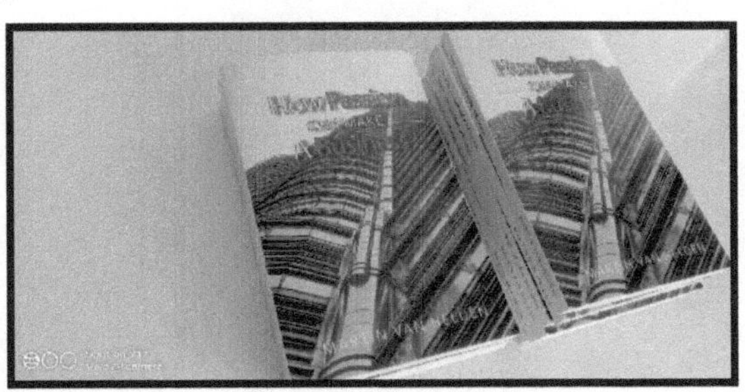

All Books are for sale at: AMAZON.com / E Bay.

www.authormartin.com

ABOUT THE AUTHOR

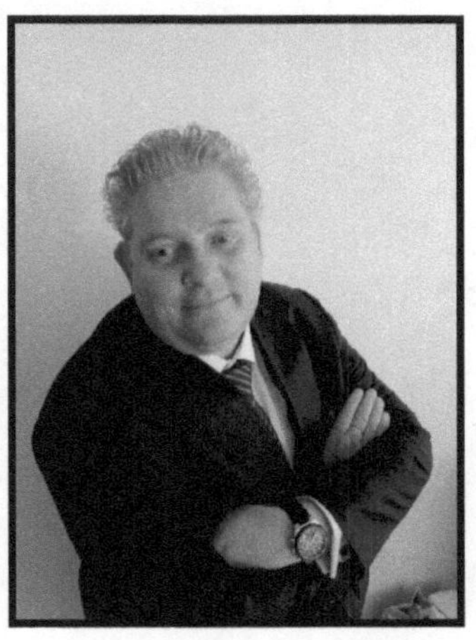

My name is Martin van Helden (post grad MBA)

AUTHOR OF AMAZING (Romantic) Thrillers and business books. My long history of owning several businesses, doing a lot of research and traveling all over the world has given me the unique Opportunity to write these amazing educating and entertaining books.

www.ingramcontent.com/pod-product-compliance
Lightning Source LLC
Chambersburg PA
CBHW062007190726
48283CB00002BA/444